CELT
AND PEPPER

CELT
AND PEPPER

RALPH McINERNY

 St. Martin's Minotaur ♔ New York

May 2013 - Fic CORE COLL ✓

www.minotaurbooks.com

Library of Congress Cataloging-in-Publication Data

McInerny, Ralph M.
    Celt and pepper : a mystery set at the University of Notre Dame / Ralph
McInerny.
        p.   cm.
    ISBN 0-312-29117-5
    1. Knight, Roger (Fictitious character)—Fiction.   2. Knight, Philip
(Fictitious character)—Fiction.   3. Private investigators—Indiana—
South Bend—Fiction.   4. University of Notre Dame—Fiction.
    5. South Bend (Ind.)—Fiction.   6. College teachers—Fiction.   I. Title.

    PS3563.A31166 C45 2002
    813'.54—dc21

                                                        2002069938

First Edition: December 2002

10   9   8   7   6   5   4   3   2   1

For Kevin and Helen Cawley

Plots were seldom original: with fair frequency, there was the irrepressible, all-betraying sneeze in the dusty attic, or the pepper flung in the assailant's eyes.

—Shirley Hazzard, GREENE ON CAPRI

CELT
AND PEPPER

PROLOGUE

WINTER IS THE SEASON WHEN the University of Notre Dame, now in the third millennium, most resembles its nineteenth-century origins. It was a bleak winter day in 1842 when Father Sorin arrived at the site of the future university and then as now a frigid wind came from the northwest and shook the leafless trees. Great drifts of snow descended from the log chapel to the frozen lake. Only a visionary could have seen a university rising from that snow-covered ground.

There are countless more buildings now and for most of the year there is incessant activity on campus. While classes are in session ten thousand students reside in the dorms and other housing provided for them; they fill the dining halls and hurry from class to class along the campus walks. In May, after the graduation ceremonies are over, there is a slight lull, punctuated only by weddings in the campus church, but before the month is out a seemingly endless series of activities enlivens the campus. Flag-twirlers gather, crash courses in Catholicism are given, charismatic rallies are held, conferences convene, thousands of kids take part in sports programs, and wistful alumni wander about the campus, trying to get their bearings in the new Notre Dame. But winter is different.

The midyear break runs from the second week in December to the third week in January, and the exodus from campus is almost total. The Morris Inn closes, the University Club shuts its doors, campus eateries keep irregular hours; the foreign student who has remained on campus, too far from home to go there, finds food difficult to get. The classrooms in DeBartolo and elsewhere are abandoned. In Decio and Molloy, the odd professor can be found in his office, but he is unlikely to answer a knock on his door. The thirteen floors of the library are all but deserted.

North of the library, beyond the intervening quartet of residence halls, two towers rise, built originally to house students, but lately converted into offices. Grace accommodates the continuing metastasis of administrative activities, Flanner houses the University Press, a center or two, but largely faculty offices. Emeriti can be found there, moving arthritically about, but several floors are occupied by active faculty, by and large independent types who eschew Decio, attracted by this location, away from the center of things—eccentric, as one might say. A reclusive philosopher, experts in Dante, random members of Celtic Studies, are quartered there. It was in an office on the seventh floor of Flanner that the body of visiting professor Martin Kilmartin was discovered one January afternoon during the midsemester break.

"Don't die between semesters," Father Carmody advised Roger Knight. "Above all, don't die in a campus office."

Prompted by the discovery of Kilmartin's corpse, the old priest had been recounting lugubrious stories of campus deaths of yore, especially when the deceased had not been discovered for some time. In one such tale, Father McAvoy, the archivist, had been found in his office in the library on a Monday, having died most likely on the previous day.

"That was quick," Father Carmody added. "There have been some others . . ." He stopped when Roger lifted a hand. "Of course Joe Evans is a special case."

"Joe Evans?"

"Director of the Jacques Maritain Center. A legendary bachelor don. But he lived off campus and was found dead in his apartment. In August. August is another bad month to die."

"What month would you recommend, Father?"

"October," Carmody said without hesitation. "Mid week in October. The funeral can be held on Saturday morning. A hundred thousand fans on campus!"

Father Carmody was of an age, eighty on his last birthday, and doubtless found thoughts of death congenial enough. Often in talking with the old priest, Roger had the sense that Carmody felt somewhat posthumous already. But events like the discovery of young Kilmartin's body revived him.

"Did you know him, Roger?"

"I had hoped to know him better. We really talked only once." Roger shook his head. "There seemed no need for haste. I love his poetry."

"He was a poet?"

"An Irish poet."

"Ah."

It was a grim thought to anyone but Father Carmody that Kilmartin's body might not have been discovered for weeks. As it was, the preliminary guess was that he had been dead for three days when a graduate student, in the building late, noticed the light under Kilmartin's door. There was no response to her knock. When the light was still on the following day she told maintenance. Even in its current affluence the university would not wish to have lights burning continually in empty offices. But the office was not empty. Branigan, in whose charge the building was, stood before the locked door of Kilmartin's office and glanced at the graduate student, an intense young woman named Melissa Shaw.

"What's that smell?"

She had no idea. Branigan grew wary and decided to call campus security. Thus, when the door was opened three people discovered the body: the custodian, Melissa Shaw, and a pudgy uniformed woman who had come across campus by bicycle.

"It was like entering a mausoleum," Branigan said later.

"Go on," the reporter said.

"Like violating a grave. Know what I mean?"

If the reporter knew, her response was not recorded. "But you went in?"

This was a touchy point with Branigan. When he unlocked the door, Katie Schwenk, the campus cop, took one glance inside, put her right arm across her eyes, and barred the doorway with the other.

"Call the police," she snapped at Branigan.

"I already did."

She meant the real police. Campus security had limited jurisdiction and certainly was not equipped to handle dead bodies. While they waited, Katie hung up the phone that lay on the desk and then stood guard at the closed office door, Melissa was sick in the ladies room and Branigan went downstairs to waylay the real police and exercise some authority.

It was Melissa who brought the dread news to Roger Knight. It would not be right to think, as Roger himself did, that given the all but deserted campus she had come to him because there was no one else she could tell. She had audited his course on the twelfth century in the just-ended fall semester, drawn by his promise to discuss Bernard of Clairvaux's life of St. Malachy. It is widely thought that the saintly Cistercian was an early victim of Irish blarney, passing on to his reader the wild tales about Ireland Malachy had told him. Roger wasn't so sure that the saint could have been so easily duped, even by another saint. A week had sufficed for the discussion but Melissa stayed on for the meetings Roger devoted to St. Anselm. It had been through Melissa that he had his first meeting with Martin Kilmartin.

"Are you reading that?" Melissa asked one day in his office, pointing to a book on Roger's desk.

"Do you know it?"

"He's visiting here, you know. Kilmartin. The author. I'm taking his class."

"And what class is that?"

"Writing Poetry." Melissa blushed. "I couldn't write a Hallmark card, but I took the course anyway."

Roger was surprised to hear that the poet was at Notre Dame. It was a sad thought, a poet like Kilmartin giving classes to students who couldn't aspire even to writing greeting card verse. There was no indication on the book's dust jacket that Kilmartin taught at Notre Dame, of course, and in any case Roger was reading his first volume, published five years before. It turned out that Kilmartin was newer to the campus than Roger himself, here on a visiting appointment.

"Why are the Irish such masters of English?" Roger asked Kilmartin when the introductions were over. They were seated on one of the benches that lined the campus walks, theirs in the shadow of Flanner. The bench easily accommodated the massive Roger Knight and the exiguous Kilmartin.

"The revenge of the conquered." Kilmartin smiled as if he were trying to conceal his snaggled teeth. He had pale blue eyes and thin unruly hair and a complexion that might never have seen the sun. The smile was more engaging when he forgot about his teeth. They fitted the face. The face of a poet.

"Did you teach somewhere else before coming here?"

"Good God, no. I'm a poet not a professor."

In Dublin he had done this and that, some reviewing, and he had won a prize that kept him for a time. When the director of Celtic Studies at Notre Dame, a Dublin native herself, offered Kilmartin a visiting professorship, he thought, why not?

"I've never had so much money in my life."

"The laborer is worthy of his hire."

"Laborer! I teach two days a week."

He taught a course in Yeats as well as the class for aspiring poets. Kilmartin was not sure that he approved of what he had been hired to do. "Whoever heard of becoming a poet by taking lessons?"

"Poetae nascuntur?"

"What's that mean?"

"Poets are born."

"Latin?"

"Yes."

"I gave a Latin title to one of my poems."

"Dies Irae."

"You know it?"

Roger threw back his head, consulted the clouds, and began.

> *Every day of his life came down to this,*
> *his last, whose sun has set,*
> *and quick time into the dark he steps to bliss*
> *or doom. Each deed, each unpaid debt,*
> *each meager merit too, now sums him up*
> *for good and all. The last trump*
> *blew everything else away except*
> *the self he shaped. What's done is kept . . .*

Kilmartin interrupted. "Every time I see or hear a poem of mine I want to change it."

"Don't change *Dies Irae*."

Well, he would never change it now.

PART ONE

1 THE DIRECTOR OF CELTIC STU-
dies was in Dublin on leave and during her
absence Padraig Maloney was grudgingly sitting in for her. He called
the director Pope Joan and compared himself to the cardinal that
took charge while a consistory was held to elect a new pontiff.
Melissa Shaw was Maloney's student assistant as well as unofficial
den mother of undergraduate students in the program. It was in this
latter role that she had kidded Arne Jensen during registration the
previous August.

"Your mother Irish?" she asked him.

"She was born in Copenhagen."

"So how come Celtic Studies?

"Because I'm Danish."

"I don't get it."

"Don't you know that Dublin was founded by the Vikings?"

Melissa just stared at him. Later she learned that it wasn't as wild
a remark as it had sounded. Padraig Maloney, acting chair of the
program, asked to see Jensen.

"You want to take my course in Irish Drama?"

"Is it closed?"

"No, no. Melissa told me what you said about Dublin."

Arne was six feet tall with straight blond hair and unblinking blue
eyes. He was listed as preprofessional, which suggested an over-
achiever. "It's true, isn't it, Professor? The Vikings founded Dublin."

"Do you want it back?"

A slight delay, then two sparkling rows of teeth were put on display
in a smile.

"When the Irish give back the English language."

With sound views like those, how could Arne be refused admission to any course offered by Celtic Studies? Maloney almost wished he had refused, though, when the young Viking said he also wanted to take Martin Kilmartin's poetry writing course, offered through Celtic Studies but cross-listed in English as well, an unfair advantage. Jensen would give Kilmartin's a higher enrollment than Maloney's course. There was a rivalry between them, declared and waged in the privacy of Maloney's mind, although obvious to Melissa. She also knew that the real prize was Deirdre Lacey, not class enrollment.

Kilmartin had learned the hard way that smoking was not permitted in Flanner. Thanks to the trendsetters in the main building, the whole campus was smoke-free and this forced the well-behaved to step outside into the cold and freeze their lungs while giving them a new coat of nicotine. A savage practice. Half the occupants of the seventh floor of Flanner smoked so the hardship was widely felt.

"We should apply for an exemption."

"Could smoking count as a species of handicap?"

"You'd need a letter from your doctor."

"We ought to have a special parking space at least."

"I'd almost settle for that," Kilmartin said.

When he went out for a smoke he sat in his parked car, sheltered from the cold. It was thus that his advantage with Deirdre had increased, all the more impressive because she was the one person in the program who did not smoke. Still she went off with the poet to his car when he craved a cigarette. Padraig Maloney asked Melissa to find out if Deirdre understood the dangers of secondhand smoke.

It made Melissa feel older to watch the doomed campaign Padraig Maloney waged for Deirdre. Why was Maloney the only one who couldn't see she was not for him? He was a bear of a man, tall and overweight, with a red and shapeless beard. He squinted at the world through the cloudy lenses of thick glasses. His voice was that of an angel, and when he taught he enacted all the parts of the play being read. A virtuoso performance. His brogue was more pronounced than anyone else's in the program, but that was acting too. He had been born in Peoria and had not even seen Ireland until he was a graduate student. He very nearly never came back. Over the transatlantic telephone he put the question to his father, "Why in God's name did you ever leave?"

Well, why did anyone ever leave Ireland except to keep body and soul together? A lack of potatoes or a lack of jobs came down to the same thing. Patrick Maloney had gone to the New World and prospered, raising five others beside Padraig. His brothers and sisters plugged their ears when Padraig talked of Ireland, but their father had bought a small farm in County Clare to which he and their mother Kathleen could retire when the time came.

"Over my dead body," Mrs. Maloney cried when he revealed the purchase to her. "I'll not live in that cold rainy country again. Florida or Arizona, yes, but County Clare? You must be out of your mind."

Kathleen was from Clare, the town of Ennis, and Patrick had thought the location of the farm would trump her sour memories of the old country. *I'll take you home again, Kathleen?*

Padraig's parents now wintered in Sarasota and the farm in Clare was rented out.

"Will you inherit the farm?" Melissa asked him.

"A sixth of it maybe." His eyes drifted to the window and he sighed as if a vision of a little farm in Clare had formed upon the pane.

He was forty-five and unmarried, in the Irish way, but belatedly he had become susceptible to the charms of Deirdre Lacey, nearly twenty years his junior, who responded to him as she would to an older brother, or even an uncle. It did not seem to occur to her that his manner meant anything amorous. One day he took her hand and kissed it. He continued to hold it in both of his and looked pleadingly at her through his wild brows.

"What's this?"

"Deirdre . . ." All fluency fled in these unprecedented circumstances. His head was chock-full of lines that could have been spoken, lines written by others and often delivered by Maloney to rooms full of rapt students, but this was not make-believe and he had no words of his own for the occasion. Deirdre tugged her hand free.

He blurted out, " 'Only God could love you for yourself alone and not your yellow hair.' "

It was the best he could do. He had to say something. Deirdre's hair was jet black, unlike Lady Anne Gregory's, the target of Yeats's poem. It had the effect of neutralizing the scene.

"I love that line," Deirdre cried. She decided that Padraig had just been acting, that kissing her hand had been only a bit of stage business.

"You should dye your hair," he said.

"Just for you."

And that was it. Melissa, eavesdropping from the outer office, felt her heart break for poor Padraig. Later he looked out his office window and saw Kilmartin hand Deirdre into his parked car in the lot below. The car remained parked. Wisps of smoke emerged from the cracked window on the driver's side.

"They're having a smoke," Melissa explained, joining him at the window.

"But she doesn't smoke."

"Where there's fire . . ."

He turned to her angrily. "What the hell is that supposed to mean?"

Melissa retreated, but later, she was glad she had given him advance warning. Anyone with eyes to see knew about Kilmartin and Deirdre. Arne Jensen knew.

"She must be crazy," Arne said.

"What have you got against Kilmartin?"

"He's a poet. You should remind her of the wives of poets."

This was odd coming from Arne, who was in Kilmartin's poetry writing course and kept a notebook he refused to let Melissa see.

"I show you mine."

"You've been at it for a while."

"But first things are often best."

He hugged his notebook to his chest, preventing her from taking it. Was she really that interested? After classes began, he kept dropping by the office of Celtic Studies to talk to her. She was a year older than he was. She hoped he didn't think she was even older than that since he was a senior and she was a second-year graduate student. Precocious but not a prodigy. He seemed not to think about it, nor did she, until she accepted first an invitation to lunch at the eatery in Grace, the building next to Flanner, and then a night at a sports bar to watch Notre Dame play at Nebraska. The unseen notebook made her curious.

"So when do I see your poems?"

He actually looked around to see if she had been heard. Well, he had to be careful. He would be going to medical school in the fall. He was not ashamed that he liked poetry, he just didn't want anyone to know that he was trying to write it too. Of course he had to hand things in to Kilmartin.

It was the poet's ego-shattering practice to read student work to the class and comment on it, anonymously, of course, but the idea was that everyone could profit from what he had to say about a particular effort. Presumably nobody other than the author knew whose work Kilmartin was dissecting, but when Arne's came up, Melissa was sure it was his. For one thing, his face was suffused in a blush before he brought both hands like blinkers to the sides of his face.

Your honeyed appellation is sweet upon my ear.

Having read the line once, Kilmartin paused, then read it again, just the one line. There was a stirring among the students. The next time he read it, there was a muffled laugh.

"None of that now," Kilmartin said, but his eyes were merry. "Let's talk about this line."

He talked about it for forty-five minutes, commenting on the use of so recherché a term as "appellation" and calling attention to the rhythm of the line. Ta tum ta ta ta tum ta ta tum ta ta ta tum. Is that how it should be scanned? Or was it a variation on iambic pentameter? Perhaps it could be read as an Alexandrine? The single line was all the text he needed for all this. And more.

"A problematical line here or there may be unavoidable. May be. I doubt it. You must know the rhythm of your lines."

Kilmartin's assignments stressed writing in demanding forms. Triolets for starters, then more complicated ones, villanelles, sonnets, Shakespearian and Petrarchan. As Melissa explained to Arne, even if you never wrote a decent poem yourself, you would begin to understand poetry from the poet's point of view and that was priceless.

He made a face. "From one poet's point of view anyway."

If she'd had any doubt that the single line dissected was Arne's, that peevish remark would have removed it. A week later she managed to peek into his notebook. He sat beside her in class and normally shielded it from view, but a threatened sneeze sent his hand in search of his handkerchief and the line Kilmartin had analyzed stood solitary on the page. Under a single word, apparently the title. Melissa.

Her breath caught. Good grief, was he writing a poem to her? After Kilmartin's analysis the line was stamped on her memory but she would have retained it anyway, guessing that it was Arne's. She was dying to ask him about it, but she couldn't. The sneeze never happened, his notebook was again shielded from her sight. She found it oddly exhilarating that someone had even started a poem about her. Suddenly she felt a new tenderness toward the tall blue-eyed future physician.

Under "Melissa" in the dictionary is to be found: "1. *Class. Myth.* The sister of Amalthea who nourished the infant Zeus with honey." In Greek *melissa* means "bee," in Latin "honey." Had Arne looked it up, was that the explanation of his line? Melissa now found it to be a wonderful line. Later in the Huddle, under the roar of voices, she murmured, "Your honeyed appellation is sweet upon my ear." Arne leaned forward and cupped his ear. She repeated it. Blood rushed to his face and he stared at her.

"I like it," she said.

He shrugged. He wanted to pretend the line was not his. But she knew better. She felt like his muse when they crossed the campus to the dining hall.

Back in Flanner, when Melissa returned from the Huddle, Professor Maloney informed her with an air in which triumph warred with indifference that he had been invited to have breakfast on the morning of the game with the president.

"Is the *president* coming?"

"Of the university!" Her misunderstanding robbed the announcement of its importance.

"But what's it all about?"

"Damned if I know."

2 ⟶ J A M E S   E L L I O T   '7 6   H A D   M A-
jored in economics, learning everything he had
to forget in order to make a success of the business he had nurtured
from idea to affluence. ELLIOT'S WASTE was one of several that com-
peted for the trash business in central Michigan. The business made
a quantum jump when Elliot, anticipating the rage for recycling, had
outbid his competitors in the suburban market. With nine locations
and twelve fleets of trucks, Elliot's vehicles rolled through the sub-
urbs at the crack of dawn, their crews meeting the demanding schedule set them as they gathered up the debris that is a major product
of an affluent civilization. He had toyed with the idea of calling the
business ELLIOT'S GARBAGGIO but his wife Diane had nixed that.

"You're not Italian."

"Is garbaggio Italian?"

"Just call it what it is."

"A garbage business."

"A waste business."

A rose by any other name, Elliot figured, not voicing the thought
Diane had not reacted negatively when he hit on ELLIOT'S WASTE as
the name of the firm. The allusion was intended. At Notre Dame, he
had taken a course from Malachy O'Neill, a legendary professor of
English, worthy successor to the sainted Frank O'Malley. Just getting
into that course had represented a triumph and he was predisposed
to be impressed. There were students who spent four years at Notre
Dame trying unsuccessfully to be admitted to O'Neill's course in
Catholic Writers. Elliot had not left matters to chance.

"I knew your father," O'Neill said when Elliot got next to him at the bar in the Morris Inn and introduced himself. O'Neill lived on campus, in an apartment over the original art museum. He ate on campus, he slept on campus, he taught on campus, he spent hours in the pay café in the South Dining Hall, whiling away the time with groups of admiring undergraduates. At Christmas, he boarded the South Shore to Chicago to be with his sister. During the long summer vacation, he took up his station on the shore of St. Joseph's lake, where he unfolded his beach chair beneath an umbrella and, with a thermos of gin and tonic within reach, reread the authors he loved.

"But my father graduated in 1958," James Elliot had said, and as soon as he said it he was sorry. O'Neill turned pale gray eyes on him.

"We were undergraduates together. I graduated in '61," O'Neill murmured. "I was not suggesting that I taught your father. But I knew him. I remember him."

"I want to get into your course."

"Why?"

"It can't be as good as they say."

"It isn't. What's your major?"

A second moment of truth when he might have lied. But he didn't. "Economics."

O'Neill nodded. Elliot was to learn that O'Neill did not favor English majors. Like graduate students, they tended to hold him in disdain. O'Neill's contagious enthusiasm for the authors he discussed seemed unprofessional to those who hoped to make a career out of rendering literature unpalatable.

"Literature is not a specialty," O'Neill would often repeat. "Specialists despised Dickens in his day."

But the major reason for the negative judgment of O'Neill was that he never published.

"My job is to teach the students in front of me, not address anonymous strangers in print."

After James Elliot succeeded in being admitted to O'Neill's course, he felt a small letdown. How would he do in such a course? He had been humbled by philosophy and had his faith tested by theology.

The only reason he was in the Arts College was that Economics was located there. He had thought of switching to business, but his father vetoed that.

"You'd be fighting the last war."

"In the business school?"

"A manner of speaking. Generals fight old wars. Business schools teach outmoded methods. Stay where you are."

He asked his father, "Do you remember Malachy O'Neill?"

"The tennis player?"

"Did he play tennis?"

"He did when I knew him."

O'Neill was a spare man of middle height, always impeccably dressed, pale red hair rising from his forehead in a series of waves that gave him a Woody the Woodpecker look from the side. It was barely possible to imagine him on the tennis courts in the past, but O'Neill had been abusing his body for decades and avoided all exercise but walking. Guesses were made on the number of cigarettes he smoked in the course of the day. He smoked everywhere but in church, and his average for a fifty-minute class was seven Pall Malls. It was in O'Neill's class that James was introduced to *The Wasteland*.

"T. S. Eliot is a Catholic author," O'Neill decreed. "He's more Catholic than Joyce."

Reading Joyce's *Portrait of the Artist* with O'Neill was an unforgettable experience. The course made an indelible impression on James Elliot, fostering a love of literature that only increased with the years. He bought first editions of the authors he loved, but he preferred reading them in paperback editions. Now in his fifties, his four children grown—the youngest a junior at Notre Dame—he had more money than he would ever need and stood to make a great deal more if he sold his business to a conglomerate that was out to monopolize the trash business in the Midwest. In any case, the business now ran itself. His son William was his less than enthusiastic successor and was in favor of selling ELLIOT WASTE to MIDSTATES REMOVALS. There was a small family foundation, managed by his son

Gregory. His daughter Dolores had married a physician and young Brian had said he wanted to be a priest. Of course that was some years ago.

It was James Elliot's regret that none of his children had been able to take a class taught by Malachy O'Neill. The man had burned out by the time the oldest arrived on campus, alcohol and tobacco exacting their toll. One day he collapsed while lecturing on Graham Greene's *The Power and the Glory*. The funeral had been a Notre Dame event. Sacred Heart could not contain all the alumni who returned for the occasion. James Elliot was there. It was two years later that the provost called on him in his room in the Morris Inn during a football weekend, bringing along David Simmons.

"David is with the Notre Dame foundation," the provost said. "He has something he would like to talk with you about. I hope you find it interesting."

"I was in one of the last classes Malachy O'Neill taught," Simmons said.

There was the Open Sesame. James wanted all the details and Simmons supplied them, speaking with obvious warmth of the deceased professor.

"There ought to be a memorial to him," Simmons said. "Something fitting."

"What did you have in mind?"

David Simmons would not have been as successful at what he did if he gave straight answers to questions like that. The discussion had continued. James Elliot was disposed to be generous to his alma mater; he did not need to be persuaded that Malachy O'Neill should be immortalized on the campus where he had taught to such effect. They discussed a building, they discussed an endowed professorship, they discussed a Notre Dame edition of the authors O'Neill had taught. A building seemed inappropriate, but a Malachy O'Neill Chair in Catholic Literature had been established, with mixed results. Geoffrey Sauer, the person hired, was a Joyce scholar who had written an unreadable book on *Finnegan's Wake*. He was said to be translating Joyce into Esperanto, but that might have been a joke. As a teacher, he was deadly and undergraduates could not be bribed to take his courses. He was everything that Malachy O'Neill had avoided becoming. The special edition of Malachy's favorite authors was published by the university press, but James Elliot was far from satisfied that he had paid his debt to a beloved professor. "The endowed chair was a mistake."

David Simmons nodded. And waited.

"There has to be something else."

But what it would be remained undetermined. For the next year, the conversation between James Elliot and Simmons resumed whenever James was on campus.

"I think I may have it," Simmons had said in September.

"What is it?"

"Will you be here for the Michigan game?"

"Of course."

"Can you save some time for me then?"

"I intend to go to the pep rally."

"How about breakfast on Saturday morning?"

"Where?"

"In the Morris Inn. The president would like to join us."

3 THE KNIGHT BROTHERS HAD
met James Elliott in the line of duty.

Philip Knight was in some ways happier than his brother when Roger was named Huneker Professor of Catholic Studies at Notre Dame. In an electronic age, location had become virtual and Phil was running his private investigation agency out of Rye, having moved up the Hudson after being mugged a second time in Manhattan. An 800 number advertised in the yellow pages of selected cities across the nation brought him sufficient inquiries from which to choose his clients. When feasible Roger accompanied him on the cases he took, and given Roger's bulk this meant taking the specially converted van in which, unlike public transportation, Roger could be comfortable. Last August, on one of their rare excursions since moving to South Bend, they had driven up into central Michigan in response to an appeal from James Elliot. Phil was susceptible because there was a connection between Elliot's appeal and Notre Dame.

"I'm a domer," Elliot had said without preamble. Philip looked at Roger for help.

"An alumnus of Notre Dame," Roger explained. "Named from the golden dome atop the main building."

"Class of '76," Elliot said.

Of course the Knight brothers had met Notre Dame alumni before their move to the Midwest. They were acquainted with the phenomenon of the "subway alumnus," the fan who cheered on Notre Dame teams from a distance but who may never have been near the school itself. Many universities have a mystique, loyal alumni are not unknown, but there is no other school from which thousands of complete strangers award themselves honorary degrees. By contrast, the Elliot family was in its third generation at Notre Dame. There might have been a bit of a chip on James Elliot's shoulder when he mentioned the source of the family wealth to the Knights.

"Waste."

"Waste?"

"Trash. Debris. Garbage." He pointed to a map on the wall. "ELLIOT WASTE. We dominate central Michigan."

James Elliot's reason for wanting to enlist the services of a private investigator was not readily classifiable. Before agreeing to come to Michigan, Philip had determined that neither the suspected infidelity of a spouse nor a runaway child was involved. He was assured that the task was important and honorable.

"Perhaps you know of the tremendous influence Malachy O'Neill had on his students."

"I have heard stories about him," Roger said.

James Elliot shook his head impatiently. "Nothing short of knowing the man could convey the strength of his influence. What I want you to do involves Professor O'Neill."

When James Elliot eventually revealed why he had brought Philip Knight all the way to Midlothian, Michigan, silence settled over the office. Elliot wanted Phil to find out whether or not an alumnus named Weber had indeed been a student of O'Neill's and was in the classroom when the great man collapsed and died. Donald Weber was a native of Midlothian, a classmate of Elliot's who had returned to his hometown to teach on the local campus. Clearly a boyish rivalry between Weber and Elliot had survived into middle life.

"The man is my age! He was back there then as a graduate student, a retarded one, as he himself puts it. But I know O'Neill wouldn't let a graduate student into his class."

"But Weber says he was?"

"And I don't believe him."

"Can't you simply call the registrar and ask?"

"No! Weber's niece works in the registrar's office. This has to be done discreetly." Sadness descended on him. "He may be telling the truth."

It was Elliot's inflated fear that any direct inquiry by himself, or by anyone connected with himself, would be relayed to his classmate. If Weber's claim was true, Weber's advantage would be intolerably increased. If it was false, Elliot did not want his foe to be forewarned.

"Does it matter that much?"

"Oh yes. It matters. The memory of a great man should not be tainted by false claims and imagined associations."

It has been said that the intensity of academic disputes can only be appreciated when one knows the triviality of what is at stake. Perhaps the rivalries within any group seem petty and absurd to outsiders. In any case, the seriousness with which James Elliot regarded the possibly fictitious claim of Donald Weber to have been there when the great O'Neill had fallen could not be denied. The sum of money he offered for this information underscored its importance to him.

Our lives turn on contingencies. At no other time would Philip Knight have come so far without knowing what the request of a potential client was. At no other time would he have agreed to take on such an absurdly simple task. But now he was influenced by the connection with Notre Dame. Roger was now comfortably installed in the Hunneker Chair of Catholic Studies and it seemed a case of noblesse oblige. The information Elliot wanted, Philip guessed, could be obtained with a minimum of effort.

"I'll look into it as soon as we return to Notre Dame."

If James Elliot had doubted his request would be accepted he gave no sign of it.

"Tell us about Donald Weber," Roger suggested.

"You'll meet him at lunch."

Weber and Elliot had been boys together in Midlothian, they had been rivals from childhood, and they had carried their rivalry with them to South Bend. After graduation, Weber spent ten years in the Navy and when discharged he had entered graduate school on the west coast. But eventually he returned to South Bend, and in his early forties, earned a doctorate in English from Notre Dame, an achievement that earned him the prospect of professional unemployment. Ph.D.'s in English were a glut on the national market and jobs were at a premium. It had been Weber's dream to join the faculty at Notre Dame. In the event, he was fortunate to find a position in his hometown at Midlothian College.

"The lowest level of the academic inferno," he explained to Roger when it came up at table in the Midlothian Athletic Club.

"The circle of ice?"

"You have to be here in the winter."

James Elliot had the look of a professor, whereas Weber could have been the emperor of trash. The conversation was all about Notre Dame and soon turned on Weber's ill-concealed astonishment that Roger had been given an endowed chair. He quizzed Roger about his academic background, he wondered what he had been doing during these non-teaching years. To say that he was shocked by what he learned would be an understatement. His envy was palpable.

"I just don't understand," he confessed.

"You can imagine my own surprise. My little book on Baron Corvo seems to have opened the door for me."

Weber did not know who Corvo was nor did he seem anxious to learn. Roger had the distinct impression that Elliot had arranged this luncheon in order that Weber might be annoyed. Finally, the disgruntled Midlothian professor let it go. "They never hire alumni, you know."

With that as solace, he was open to Elliot's introduction of Malachy O'Neill as topic.

"I have modeled my life on his," Weber said fervently. James Elliot brought his napkin to his mouth as if to gag.

"He must have been a great teacher," Roger said.

"Incomparable. I am one of the few alumni who can boast having taken two of his courses, once as an undergraduate, again as a graduate student. I was in the classroom when he collapsed and died." He lowered his head. Across the table, James Elliot's eyes sparked with angry triumph. The Knight brothers had now heard the claim from Weber's own lips.

"The guy does seem like a phony," Phil said when they drove out of town later than day.

"Oh, I don't know," Roger said. "An enthusiast certainly."

When they returned to Notre Dame, they learned, with the discreet help of their friend Father Carmody, that Donald Weber had indeed been enrolled as an auditor in the last class taught by Malachy O'Neill.

"What's so hush hush?" the priest asked.

"It's confidential, Father. A client. . . ."

"All this fuss over poor O'Neill. What he might have been if he had only controlled his drinking we will never know."

James Elliot's reaction to the finding was one of jealous disbelief. "His niece must have altered the records. Can you find that out?"

It fell to Roger to convince James Elliot that his campaign to discredit Donald Weber was unworthy of him. And of the memory of a beloved professor.

"Weber did lie about one thing, though."

"What's that?"

"He said he had taken two courses from O'Neill. Actually, he only took the one."

"The last one?" There was anguish in Elliot's voice.

"I'm afraid so."

That disappointing discovery formed a bond between James Elliot and the Knights. The alumnus kept in touch. It was the rare campus visit that he did not look them up, and to Phil's delight he was often Elliot's guest in his choice seats on the fifty-yard line at football games. As the date of the football game with Michigan approached and Elliot had not been heard from, Philip was resigned to watching the game from his usual seat in the south end zone. But on Thursday the call came.

"Can you join me, Phil?" Elliot asked.

"Of course."

"And your brother?"

"It's really too much trouble for him to get in and out of the stadium."

Elliot sighed. "Too bad. Maybe my son Brian will join us. I have a breakfast meeting, so why don't we just meet at the stadium?"

And so it was arranged.

BUT BRIAN WOULD ATTEND the game with Melissa Shaw.

Weeks ago, Arne Jensen had told Brian about Melissa and had pointed her out on campus before introducing Brian to her in Reckers. That had been a fateful mistake on Arne's part. Not only did Brian understand Arne's fascination with Melissa; almost immediately he shared it. He secretly signed up for a course on the Celtic Twilight when he learned Melissa would be sitting in. Infatuation had been fed by proximity. Could this be love?

Brian sought lofty parallels to his plight. Dante had been led out of confusion by the influence of Beatrice, Petrarch was inspired by Laura, and Scott Fitzgerald had Zelda. History is replete with stories of women who inspired unworthy males, and such precedents occurred to Brian Elliot when he followed Melissa Shaw's lead and signed up for Roger Knight's class.

His major was preprofessional, his goal was medical school, and he had no idea what a Celtic twilight might be. One glimpse of Melissa would have sufficed to justify this waste of three credits. Here was a woman worthy of sonnets. No need to warn Arne of his interest in Melissa, of course. His excuse to his friend was boredom with the exact sciences. And the fact that his father had urged him to take a class from Roger Knight. Thus Brian had assured himself of a semester's proximity to the lovely Melissa. It would have been ideal if it had not been for the imposing Nordic presence of Arne Jensen, who was also taking the class and was helpless to conceal the fact that he found Melissa at least as powerful an attraction as the massive Roger Knight.

"Sometimes I think I have a vocation," Brian said to Melissa in early September. He had long ago outgrown his boyish dream of becoming a priest but had discovered that a feigned attraction to celibacy was a powerful aphrodisiac with young women.

"Vocation to what?"

"Maybe the monastery."

"What do you think of Joyce?" Melissa asked Brian.

"I don't know her."

Had female laughter ever seemed as golden as hers? She took his remark for a witticism and he did not correct her. It was intimidating to learn that she was a graduate student.

"I'm young for my age," she said.

"Tell me about it."

He led her away to the restaurant in Grace Hall, where she wouldn't let him pay for her food.

"Don't be silly," she said.

But she told him about graduate studies and what she hoped to do with her life. He was acquainted with women aiming at a career, the business school was full of them, but her ambitions were different. Her dream was to live and die on such a campus as this. All Brian could think was what a waste it would be if her dream was realized.

"You were kidding about James Joyce, weren't you?"

"Up to a point."

"Tell me about yourself."

Had any biographical sketch ever seemed so dull? He skidded over the fact that he was from Midlothian, Michigan; of course he did not mention that his family was affluent or how they had gotten that way. But she seemed impressed when he mentioned medical school as she had not been when he tried the priestly vocation line on her.

"How did you wind up in Celtic Twilight?"

He wasn't about to tell the whole truth. "Someone recommended Professor Knight."

His father, whose romantic memories of his time at Notre Dame seemed to evoke a past that no longer existed. Thank God his father

30

had not attached the family name to any of his benefactions to the university.

"Are you related to James Elliot?" Roger Knight asked him after the first meeting of the class.

"He's my father."

"I've met him."

"He told me."

"He and my brother have become good friends."

He would have been made uneasy by the overweight professor's remarks if Melissa had not shown interest in this surprising connection. His father was delighted when he told him he was taking a class from Roger Knight.

"Good. Good. Now that's my idea of a professor."

"He says you know his brother."

"He told you that?" His father seemed wary.

"Don't you?"

"I know them both."

It was a further bonus of Roger Knight's remark that it seemed to give him an advantage over Arne Jensen. Melissa was glad to grant his request that she help him with the course.

"I have trouble understanding poetry."

She smiled indulgently. "Yeats isn't difficult."

"Maybe not for you."

The smile grew warmer. "You remind me of my brother."

That was bad but what could he say? "I thought Arne was your brother."

"He wants to be a poet."

"Come on."

"So do I."

"You write poetry?"

"I try. The two of us are in another class together."

This called for a quick switch of topic. "Are you going to the game Saturday?"

"The game?"

"Michigan–Notre Dame."

"I've never been inside the stadium."

He allowed for a moment of silence but she hadn't meant to be sacrilegious. "Would you like to go?"

He might have suggested that she make a journey to the North Pole. But, unfamiliar as she apparently found it, she began to show interest. "But I don't have a ticket."

"I'll get you one. We can sit in the student section."

She agreed. He arranged to pick her up for the pep rally Friday night as well, and that gained him knowledge of where she lived, in graduate student housing east of Hesburgh Library.

"You must be able to hear the roar from the stadium during home games."

"It's not so bad. With all the people around, I usually just stay in."

(5) ROGER KNIGHT PARTICULARLY
valued his friendship with Greg Whelan, assistant university archivist. For one thing he was good company while Phil was off watching one athletic contest or another on campus, but that was simply an extra bonus of having such a knowledgeable friend. Whelan's stammer was a handicap that had blighted both his university and legal careers, but he had finally found his niche as a librarian and spent his days surrounded by precious archival material.

"Yeats visited the campus, you know," he had said to Roger.

"No, I didn't. Tell me about it."

"I'll dig out what we have."

And so it was that Roger became acquainted with the visit that William Butler Yeats had paid to Notre Dame. There was a photograph of the poet with the then president of Notre Dame, Father Charles O'Donnell, a bit of a poet in his own right. Yeats wore formal attire in which apparently he had lectured in Washington Hall. It never ceased to amaze Roger how many luminaries had found their way to the then obscure South Bend campus. That F. Marion Crawford and Henry James had lectured at Notre Dame had come as a pleasant surprise, and of course Chesterton had actually taught courses at Notre Dame. But that Yeats, an Anglo-Irishman with odd spiritualistic views, should have been feted on campus was even more surprising.

But what Greg dug out proved even more astonishing: Yeats had actually visited the campus on two occasions, once in 1903 and again thirty years later, after he had received the Nobel Prize. Greg found in *The Scholastic* an account of the three lectures given on the first occasion that was both evocative of the speaker and of the listeners, if the student journalist were any indication. Roger found himself growing more curious about Father Charles O'Donnell, who was described as president both of Notre Dame and of the Catholic Poets of America. His collected—and neglected—poems were in the Hesburgh Library.

The volume had been published by the university press in 1942, on the occasion of the centennial celebration of Notre Dame. Literary accomplishments had long since fallen out of the job description of university presidents, of course. Not that Roger could bring himself to think of O'Donnell as much of a poet, but he had his moments. His basic themes were his own priesthood and his Irish roots.

> *The hills of Donegal are green,*
> *And blue the bending sky,—*
> *For sky and hills I have not seen*
> *The holiest love have I.*

O'Donnell died in 1934, aged forty-nine. The book and the poems it contained evoked a Notre Dame that in one sense was no more but in another was ever present. With Greg Whelan beside him, Roger drove his golf cart up the road from the Grotto to the community cemetery and found the grave of Charles O'Donnell, C.S.C. From the campus came the sounds of the marching band getting ready for the big game the following day with Michigan. The Fighting Irish that had engaged the heart of O'Donnell and others on this campus long ago were not athletes but patriots struggling against the English oppressor. On his first visit to campus Yeats had spoken as much as a representative of Irish independence as a poet.

Overhead, private jets descended at regular intervals toward the airport, which bore the hybrid neologism of Michiana, affluent fans arriving for the big game. When he and Greg returned from the community cemetery, Roger took the road that led behind the Main Building, a mistake. The walks were crowded with early visitors who were in no hurry.

"Come over tomorrow afternoon," Roger said.

"Will you have the game on?"

"Of course!"

Greg was a fervent fan although he seldom attended games, preferring them televised. "I find it easier to follow then."

The game itself was not the sole reason for being in the stadium and thousands of distractions drew the less than dedicated eye from the play on the field. For Roger, the stadium represented too many challenges to his mobility. To say nothing of the fact that the amount of seat allotted each fan was woefully inadequate to his *derrière*. Better to make a huge batch of popcorn and watch at leisure in the apartment. The roar audible from the stadium added authenticity to the experience. The road along which they came was flanked by the trees that might have inspired the priest-poet-president in the lines called simply "To Notre Dame."

So well I love these woods I half believe
There is an intimate fellowship we share;
So many years we breathed the same brave air,
Kept spring in common, and were one to grieve
Summer's undoing, saw the fall bereave
Us both of beauty, together learned to bear
The weight of winter:—when I go otherwhere—
An unreturning journey—I would leave
Some whisper of a song in these old oaks,
A footfall lingering till some distant summer
Another singer down these paths may stray—
The destined one a golden future cloaks—
And he may love them, too, this graced newcomer,
And may remember that I passed his way.

Father O'Donnell had been granted his wish that day when Roger and Greg recalled his passage—if either could be called a "graced newcomer."

"Phil is going to the game?"

"Need you ask?"

Doubtless Phil would bring Father Carmody back with him afterward. Roger planned to make spaghetti and a gargantuan salad. Although Phil would be sitting with James Elliot, they would be parting after the game. Elliot always had multiple fish to fry when he was on campus.

"He still thinks Weber's niece altered the records, putting his old nemesis into O'Neill's final course."

"What would count as disproof?"

Phil laughed. "You may be right."

6 ARNE JENSEN CONFRONTED his tormentor in his Flanner office. The cork board on the wall of Martin Kilmartin's office held three darts. A fourth had lost its grip and fallen to the floor. Their target seemed to be a photograph affixed to the board.

"That's Ennis, whence I come," Kilmartin said, his tone elegiac. He looked up at Arne Jensen through a tangle of brows. "Take a pew."

The frail poet sat at a large U-shaped metal desk that matched the file cabinets against the wall. His chair had arms that swung out and raised and lowered. Kilmartin continued to fuss with them.

"Don't ask me how they work. It's a damned uncomfortable chair."

Arne sat. Melissa's account of the poet's Flanner office had not prepared him for this. Whatever image he had formed of it was miles distant from this almost empty room with its metal furniture and improvised dart board. The absence of a computer was noticeable.

"I'm in your poetry course."

"I remember the face."

Not a very flattering beginning, given the small size of the course. "I turned in a single line that you were pretty rough on."

Kilmartin looked at him with a bemused smile. " 'Your honeyed appellation is sweet upon my ear?' "

"Yes."

"Well, I remembered it. Forgetting might be harder. What does it mean?"

Arne explained it to him. "Her name is Melissa. Bee. But *mel* is honey in Latin as well as Greek."

Kilmartin forgot about the arms of his chair. He looked long at Arne and began to nod. "But what's the next line?"

"I don't know."

"Come now. It's a real girl, isn't it?"

"Yes."

"And you are speaking to her." He closed his eyes. "Your honeyed appellation is sweet upon my ear. Would that your ruby lips were nectar sweet on mine." He opened his eyes. "Awful. But in keeping with yours. You should finish it. Good or bad, something begun should be finished. At least a quatrain."

"You know her."

"Who?"

"Melissa."

"Melissa Shaw? Of course I know her." Kilmartin sat up in his chair and his manner altered. "A lovely young woman." He paused. "She's a graduate student."

This was all wrong, Arne knew it, and could not now extricate himself from the ridiculous situation of discussing Melissa with this foppish poet. Kilmartin now knew his feelings for Melissa, but what were Kilmartin's own? Maybe he was used to young women like Melissa doting on him.

"Are you a graduate student?"

Arne shook his head. "Preprofessional."

"Still an amateur?" His snaggled teeth appeared in a smile and then he began to cough. He sat still in the chair and tried to reduce the cough to a clearing of the throat. His eyes were wide as he stared at the dartboard. After a minute, it seemed over.

"I'm as fragile as a goddamn doll. Do you know Dorothy Parker? 'It's not the cough that carries you off but the coffin they carry you off in?' A cough could carry me off."

"What's wrong?"

A radiant smile. "They call it an enlarged heart. Isn't that lovely? It would seem the promise of longevity rather than a mortal threat."

"Can anything be done?"

"Yes. I can sit still, not catch cold, wear a mask like an asthmatic when pollen is in the air . . ."

No wonder Melissa was smitten with the man. Despite himself, Arne felt a surge of sympathy for the delicate poet. How could you think of a man whose days were numbered as a rival? But he still seethed because of the fun Kilmartin had had with that stupid line.

Like the course in writing poetry, Melissa represented a departure from the Arne Jensen he thought he was. A lower-middle-class family in Mound, Minnesota, his father on the county highway department, his mother a stolid woman who kept a spick-and-span house but who once had unaccountably gone off to Mankato for three days, just boarding the bus and leaving. A one-way ticket. But she came back, and that was the end of it. Had the wide world disappointed her? Her other children she understood, Arne was a puzzle. Teachers came and talked to his parents about his potential. His father considered learning an affectation, his mother sometimes seemed to think she had picked up the wrong baby at the hospital. He had his choice of colleges and chose Notre Dame, mildly shocking his Lutheran parents.

"Be careful," his father warned.

His mother hugged him as if she did not expect to see him again. He drove himself to South Bend in the Jeep he had bought with summer earnings spraying wild marijuana plants for the county highway department. He harvested some too and cured the leaves and tried to smoke them. Nothing. His plan was to go through the medical school of the University of Minnesota and then get a residency at the Mayo Clinic in Rochester. He had been reading medical books since high school. Sitting in Kilmartin's office, studying the poet, making his diagnosis, he wondered why no one had ever suggested surgery.

"So finish the poem," Kilmartin said.

"I will." Arne rose. "This is all confidential, isn't it?"

"Confidential?"

"About Melissa."

"Haven't you told her?"

Blushing was his cross. He avoided the poet's eyes.

"Not yet."

"Someone might get there before you."

A mean and merry little smile. Arne glared at him and then left, closing the door emphatically behind him.

7 FROM DOZENS OF GRILLS around the campus wisps of smoke and an alluring fragrance rose as hamburgers and hot dogs sizzled like burnt offerings to whatever angel decides the outcome of athletic contests. The closeness of Ann Arbor ensured that there would be Michigan fans in great numbers. It was an old and honorable rivalry and seasoned fans on both sides had known both heartbreak and triumph. Before the season began this game had been touted as the contest that would decide the national championship, but many things had gone wrong for both teams since then. It would be too much to say that the season of either team was ruined. Only high expectations could explain why identical 7–2 records were considered disastrous. Sportswriters wrote of the coming contest as if it were a consolation match, and there were fair-weather fans on either side who repeated such lugubrious comments. But the true blue—and the true blue and gold—fan knew otherwise. The outcome of the Notre Dame–Michigan game would decide which on this afternoon was the better team, if not the best in the nation.

At the Morris Inn, in Sorin's restaurant, James Elliot was at table with David Simmons, one of the platoon of university fund-raisers. The president had spent ten minutes with them and then gone on to stop at other tables where similar appeals were being made to the generosity of past and future benefactors of the university. Also at table was Padraig Maloney, the bearded acting director of Celtic Studies, a man to whom the president had had to be introduced and who scarcely looked up from his Eggs Benedict to acknowledge the presidential presence. Elliot's eyes met David's and there was the beginning of doubt in the benefactor's eyes. Maloney had arrived at the Morris Inn in response to the invitation to the director of Celtic Studies.

"She's on leave."

"Leave!"

"Dublin." Maloney opened the menu and began to study it greedily.

The purpose of the breakfast was to put before James Elliot a plan for a fitting tribute to the late and beloved Malachy O'Neill. A starker contrast between the formal, always well-groomed if never entirely sober professor of yore and the scruffy specimen across the table could not be imagined. David was beginning to wonder how he could indicate to Elliot that his proposal had nothing to do with this rough diamond. So why were they having breakfast with him?

"Tell me about Celtic Studies," Elliot said to Maloney.

The account was fluent but unintelligible. Once Maloney began speaking there seemed no end to the words that poured from his whiskered lips, buttery words, words unreliable, words from which all sincerity had been drained to be replaced by a jovial condescension. Maloney might have been enlisting him in a pact to defraud the university and its students.

"Such programs are all the rage, of course. Think of it as Black Studies for the third millennium. All we really do is cluster a few courses and professors and provide some semblance of a coherent effort. There is after all American Studies, a contribution of the Soviets, by the way."

"Here?"

"It's been here for years," David said, not meeting Elliot's eyes. "He means the Russians pioneered the notion of area studies."

Maloney rubbed the tip of his nose with the back of his hand and gave Elliot a devilish look. "There's even talk of a program in Catholic Studies."

"Is that right?"

"What a laugh. Catholic Studies at Notre Dame. Coals to Newcastle."

David pushed back more than slightly from the table, dissociating himself further from the chortling cynicism of Padraig Maloney, whose mellifluous voice turned the university's effort to educate the young into a chaotic scramble to disguise the fact that it didn't know what an education is. A fleeting allusion to James Joyce caused the flow to stop when Elliot asked Maloney for his view of *Finnegan's Wake.*

"It's what you will, of course. Joyce himself didn't know what he was writing half the time. How could he, the man was forever drunk. Still, one can have great fun with it."

"I was taught that it intimates Joyce's doubts about leaving the church."

Maloney roared. Eventually under control, he leaned toward Elliot with tears of laughter still leaking from his eyes. "Someone was pulling your leg, lad."

There was twenty more minutes of the man but finally they were in the lobby where Maloney stuck to them like flypaper in a comic strip, his wet red eye following the traffic into the bar. Twice David had given the professor a valedictory handshake but still he stood planted before them.

"The bar is open," Maloney observed.

"Go ahead," David said. "We may join you."

When Maloney waded into the crowd, they fled for the stairs and went up to Elliot's room, where David groaned aloud as he shut the door behind them.

"James, I can't tell you how sorry . . ."

But Elliot was oddly calm. He had seen a parody of his remembered Notre Dame, one far worse than he could have imagined. All he need do is juxtapose the elegant Malachy O'Neill and the boor with whom he had just breakfasted.

"That was a mistake." David said this as if he had just come to an agreement with himself.

"What was a mistake?"

David looked at him abjectly. "I won't even tell you what the point of asking that jackass to breakfast was."

"You thought I might want to support Celtic Studies."

"Maloney has no idea what we're considering. Remember, he was only a substitute for the director."

"He is a professor, isn't he?"

David wished he could deny it.

"And you thought I would be interested in supporting Celtic Studies?"

"That's out of the question."

"Is he really a charlatan?"

"James, he's a professor, yes. They all sound like that in the morning. It's an act. They hate the students, the administration, and one another." It was insane to tell him this.

"And hate what they teach?"

"Maloney isn't typical." Prolonging the postmortem would worsen the situation. David rose to go, shaking his head. "I feel as if I have already lost the game."

"Hey, we're going to win."

"Sure you don't want to sit in the presidential box?"

Elliot shook his head. "I have guests."

After the second quarter Michigan led 21–0 and gloom had settled over half the spectators despite the clear and sunny day. Overhead small aircraft moved slowly through the sky trailing advertising banners with messages about beer, food, someone's birthday, a proposal of marriage. Philip Knight was explaining earnestly to James Elliot what the Irish were going to have to do if they were going to turn the game around in the second half. Sacking the quarterback was the key.

And so it turned out to be. On Michigan's first possession, a blitz caused the quarterback to cough up the ball. An Irish player picked it up and ran for the end zone but was brought down by a heroic tackle, causing another fumble. To the relief of the Irish fans, the ball bounced out of bounds before a Michigan player could fall on it. Notre Dame retained possession and two minutes later had put 7 points on the board. A surprise squiggle kick led to a scramble for the ball and when an Irish player emerged with it the stadium erupted. The result was a field goal. 21–10. Wary of the blitz, the Michigan quarterback got off his passes more quickly. Quicker than his receivers could get into position, as it happened. An Irish back snared a pass and had nothing but open field between them and the end zone sixty yards away. It became 21–17. That was the score with which the fourth quarter began. Fourteen clocked minutes later it seemed that it would be the final score of the game. Michigan had the ball at midfield and needed only to run out the clock. The Irish called a time-out and, when play resumed, called another time-out. They had one remaining. When the teams finally lined up, the Irish had bunched players at the center of the line. At the snap, the avalanche rolled and what should have been a routine taking of the snap and genuflection by the quarterback, stopping play, incredibly resulted in a fumble. It took minutes for the officials to unstack the pile of players that formed over the ball. A hush had fallen over the stadium. And then the signal was given. Notre Dame's ball!

The clock showed less than a minute. The ball was on the Michigan forty-seven-yard line. A quick pass to the sideline took the ball to the Michigan thirty with only seconds off the clock. The next play was apparently a duplicate of the preceding and Michigan's defense converged on the wrong receiver. The ball went long and the Irish receiver, unable to advance beyond the ten, tried unsuccessfully to get out of bounds to stop the clock. Incredibly, the Irish did not call time-out. The clock ticked toward zero. Finally, the time-out was called but it was unclear whether the clock had run out before the request was made.

Time on an athletic field is not solar time. The watches on the wrists of referees and game clocks record sporadic not continuous time. Two minutes playing time can take fifteen by the sun, seconds inflate to minutes. There were but two seconds on the clock when the Irish lined up for the crucial play. Once the ball had been snapped the game would last as long as the play, no matter the clock. The ball was snapped. The Notre Dame quarterback took the ball where he stood and immediately flipped it across the goal line to his tight end. But before the ball could reach the eager hands of the Notre Dame receiver, a Michigan player's hand darted out and tipped the ball. It rose into the air, end over end, as players from both sides gathered under it. It dropped into a forest of clutching hands. Again a melee and pile-up that required minutes to unstack. An almost audible silence had fallen over the stadium. And then the call was made. A Notre Dame player had caught the deflected pass. The score was Notre Dame 23, Michigan 21. The extra point widened the margin to 3, but the game was over.

There was no triumphal celebrating by Irish fans and Michigan fans were stunned into silence. Seldom had it been clearer that a contest turns on contingencies that no amount of preparation can ready a team for. There was a winner but not a victor, and the team that had scored fewer points had not been beaten.

When Philip Knight and James Elliot emerged from the stadium in a crowd of fans decompressing from the excitement of the game, they came to a stop and looked at the great mural on the Hesburgh Library.

"Well," Elliot said, and there was indecisiveness in his manner.

"What are you going to do now?"

"I suppose I'll head back to the Morris Inn."

"Why don't you come home with me. It's only a short walk."

Elliot looked around, still indecisive. "I had half hoped to see my son Brian."

"You can call from our place."

Elliot agreed and they headed off in the direction of graduate student housing where the Knights had their apartment and where Roger and Greg Whelan seemed surprised to find that the game was over.

"Did we win, Phil?"

"Of course."

"Greg and I have been talking of William Butler Yeats's visits to campus."

"Yeats." Elliot said. "The Irish poet?"

There followed a delightful discussion that Elliot could not help contrasting with the disastrous lunch he'd had with David Simmons and the ineffable Maloney. Roger Knight was more like what a professor ought to be. No Malachy O'Neill, perhaps, but no Padraig Maloney either.

"I was introduced to Yeats by Malachy O'Neill. Not personally, of course, to his work."

"You studied with Malachy O'Neill?" Greg asked.

"I took a course from him."

"Tell us about it."

Elliot did, warming to the task because Roger Knight and Greg Whelan were so obviously interested.

8 AFTER LEAVING ELLIOT'S ROOM, Simmons came down into the lobby of the Morris Inn. Too late he saw Padraig Maloney.

"I've been waiting for you. Where's Daddy Warbucks?"

David allowed himself to be led into the bar. Strong drink might be the answer.

"How long have you been in this country?"

Maloney backed up to stare at him. "I'm a third-generation American."

So much for the hope of getting his green card revoked. "That's quite a brogue."

"I don't know what you mean," Maloney said without any effort to look sincere.

Simmons bought the professor a drink and then excused himself. He could not listen to Maloney without imagining shocked potential donors overhearing. What a disaster the breakfast had been! If he had been forewarned, he would have rejected such a substitute. Or was that only an ex post facto certainty? He wouldn't be surprised if James Elliot never took another call from him.

Ten minutes later, ensconced on a bench near the bookstore, Simmons lit what he hoped would be an anonymous cigarette and looked disinterestedly at the pedestrian traffic. Pre-game excitement was mounting but it left David Simmons untouched. Whenever he thought of the ineffable Padraig Maloney seated across the table from James Elliot, he felt like crying out in pain. Too late had come the realization that Maloney was the quintessence of everything Elliot loathed about the present-day faculty. It all went back to his romantic memories of Malachy O'Neill.

Damn Malachy O'Neill! The mythical status he had posthumously acquired in the fevered memories of former students was difficult to reconcile with the facts Simmons had amassed on the man. Father Hesburgh had once confided to Simmons that he had never understood a thing O'Neill said.

"His voice was soft. And he mumbled."

So much for the silver-tongued lecturer. That O'Neill had drunk deep and often was part of the legend, a plus rather than a minus. And he had been a chain smoker. He was the antithesis of today's typical nonsmoking, jogging, malcontent faculty member. That of course was a good part of his appeal for former students like James Elliot. And equally of course they claimed he had opened to them the life of the mind.

From somewhere through the trees came the *oompa oompa* of the band as it paraded to the stadium; the chatter of passersby, shouts, festive noises, drove the sense of defeat from David Simmons' soul. It was in times of adversity that one's true mettle was shown. He would snatch victory from the jaws of defeat. He would step over the fallen body of Padraig Maloney and resume his place at James Elliot's side. Somehow he would come up with an idea that brought together the man's profound love for Notre Dame and the limitless amounts of money he had with which to express that love.

With cigar smoke in his eyes and slurred shouting in his ears, Simmons watched the game in the back bar of the University Club, and its outcome seemed a clear moral lesson for him. A team that had been crushed in the first half managed to come back and, in the last moment, win. It was the Notre Dame way. It would be his way with James Elliot. But how?

Inspiration struck him along with the bracing fresh air when he left the University Club at six o'clock. Earlier there had been disappointment verging on despair. Then had come the O. Henry twist of the win over Michigan. Now came illumination and with it a pious awe. If he were sober, he would have gone off to one of the post-game Masses, to fulfill his obligation for the morrow. His seeming clarity of mind squeezed an impromptu prayer of thanksgiving from his pusillanimous heart. He resolved to visit the Grotto during the week and breathe an Ave there in thanksgiving.

Roger Knight! The name might have been written in smoke in the azure sky. It might have been emblazoned on a banner pulled through the heavens by a small but powerful plane. Roger Knight. Of course. The thought was so right he could not believe it had not occurred to him before. Anyone who cherished memories of the supposed poly-math Malachy O'Neill would find in Roger Knight an acceptable reincarnation of the departed hero. The occupant of the Huneker Chair of Catholic Studies had not come within the range of David Simmons' official functions. The money for the endowed chair Roger Knight held had been given without any mediation by the Notre Dame Foundation, given to old Father Carmody almost as a personal favor. A condition had been that Carmody oversee the search for the Hun-eker professor. There had been muffled laughter and an unearned sense of vindication when the credentials of Roger Knight were made known. A Princeton doctorate, no doubt, but the man had been em-ployed as a private investigator for nearly a decade, his brother's partner. It was more difficult to dismiss the monograph on Baron Corvo, given the reception it had enjoyed. Of course the faculty was furious, but the faculty is always furious.

It was impossible not to hear of the profound if undramatic impact Roger Knight had made during his few years on campus. A legend was aborning, no doubt of it. Mike Garvey had offered to enter Knight into the canon of Notre Dame saints with a puff piece but he was gently rebuked by the proposed honoree. The bitterest realization of all, now that inspiration had come, was that James Elliot himself had mentioned Knight and that his son Brian was enrolled in his class. But that was a plus not a minus!

As these thoughts churned in his head, Simmons was drifting north northeast from the club, in the direction of graduate student housing where the Knights were ensconced. The mad hope leapt in him that he could recoup his losses this very weekend, substitute Knight for the ineffable Maloney and let nature take her course. His head was not as clear as he supposed, needless to say, and opportunity might have insured a second defeat more crushing than the first. In any case, professional caution reasserted itself and while he continued on his way, it was no longer with any idea that he would approach Roger Knight immediately and discuss possibilities of the Huneker professor becoming the beneficiary of James Elliot's generosity.

Benches were everywhere on campus now, and the little village of graduate student housing, row after row of identical structures, was not bereft of them. David Simmons sat on a bench that gave him a clear if oblique look at the door of the Knight apartment. He smoked meditatively. No specific plan formed in his mind, but it did not matter. That would come. And it would be well to let some time pass so that Elliot could rinse his mental palate of the taste of Padraig Malony. In the fullness of time, Simmons would bring donor and recipient together.

Twilight came on. He nodded off. When he came awake again it was dark. His bench was illumined by a lamp and a couple frowned at him as they went by, a young woman quickened her pace and averted her eyes as she hurried past him. But on a game weekend it was difficult for any oddity to alarm. Beyond, a door opened and light spilled outward from it. It was the Knights' entryway. And then stepping into that light, unmistakable even at a distance, was James Elliot! Next, a tall figure was momentarily visible but then the doorway was filled with the enormous presence of Roger Knight. The voices that came to Simmons were indistinct, but the tones were the tones of friendship and camaraderie. The farewells were finished. Elliot was driven away. The door closed and unrelieved darkness returned. When David Simmons rose from his bench he felt that some unguent had been traced upon his forehead, that a flat blade had rested for a moment on his shoulder.

He could perhaps be forgiven for imagining that he had somehow brought Roger Knight and James Elliot together in stage one of his successful effort to extract more millions for Notre Dame from the waste king of central Michigan.

9

WHATEVER THE POINT HAD been of the breakfast in the Morris Inn it left no lasting impression on Padraig Maloney. What lingered was Simmons' question about how long he had been in the country. Did the man think he was a visitor like Martin Kilmartin? Maloney doubted that Simmons even knew who Kilmartin was. It had been a matter of surprise that the reputed whiz kid of the Notre Dame Foundation had even heard of Celtic Studies.

The program was amply endowed, thanks to the atavistic longings of Irish-Americans who, like American Jews with respect to Israel, loved their country of remote origin in inverse ratio to their desire to live there. He suspected that the generous donors who had made Celtic Studies viable would also be susceptible to appeals from the IRA. Nice acronym that, for one who knew Latin. The lovely Deirdre too had acquired along with her DNA a visceral love of the Old Sod, an affection that had all too easily transferred to the fragile and lyrical Martin Kilmartin. In matters of the heart, poetry was a weapon without equal. But Maloney had been left unarmed by God. He had drawers full of lousy verse of his own, testimony to his doomed effort to prove that anyone with Irish blood had the ear of the Muses. He could not bring it off. His lines seemed arbitrary in length, his rhymes contrived, the underlying ideas banal. He had to settle for criticism, lofty animadversions on the creative work of others, with especial reference to James Joyce. In a crowded field, he had secured a minor niche for himself by writing on Joyce's poetry. The great writer's two collections of verse betrayed no marks of Modernism. *Chamber Music* was traditional in both prosody and outlook. *Pomes*

Pennyeach was simple and disciplined, frothy but memorable. Even the title was self-deprecating, as if to signal that this was Joyce in a minor key, running on half a cylinder at most. Kilmartin, the arrogant bastard, condescended even to Joyce. As for Cavanaugh and Heaney . . .

"The key to becoming an Irish poet is to forget you're Irish."

"You're not serious."

"You sound like Deirdre." Kilmartin looked slyly at him.

"I've got a cold."

The essence of humor is surprise, but it was Kilmartin's response to his joke that surprised Maloney. The poet just stared and then his mouth opened slowly and the laughter began, an odd barking laughter. Kilmartin seemed to find his own laughter contagious and it fed on itself. He hugged himself, making a seatbelt out of his arms, squeezing his eyes shut so that tears ran down his pallid face.

Just as suddenly, the poet's laughter changed. He began to gasp, his eyes looked wildly at Maloney, and he pointed at his chest. Then he bent forward. Padraig sprang beside Kilmartin's chair and thumped him on the back, hard. The poet gasped. Maloney thumped him again. Kilmartin dipped forward until his forehead rested on his desk. Silence. And then a raspy breath, and another. Slowly Kilmartin sat up.

"Dear Jesus, you might have killed me, but it seems to have had the opposite effect."

"You want me to get someone? A doctor?"

Kilmartin waved away the suggestion. "Paddy, I know what they would tell me before they opened their mouths. They would tell me to quit smoking and drinking and everything else that makes life worthwhile. Isn't it a fix to be in though, a laugh or a sneeze a mortal danger?"

"Do you take any medicine?"

"I do, I do." He slid open a drawer and brought out a bottle of Jameson's. "You'll join me?"

It was like joining the condemned in a final cigarette. Maloney did that too, lighting up despite the fact that he did not smoke. Keeping Kilmartin company, that was the idea. How could he be jealous of someone as fragile as Martin Kilmartin, whose life could be snuffed out by a joke?

10

"I THOUGHT YOU WEREN'T IN-terested in football," Arne said accusingly.

He had heard she had gone to the game with Brian, perhaps from Brian. There was a fleeting pleasure in the thought of two young men vying for her favors, but Melissa's sights were set higher. For reasons that might baffle a psychiatrist but which any grandmother would have guessed, she began to speak of Padraig Maloney's crush on Deirdre, but her manner warned him not to laugh.

"She seems more interested in Kilmartin."

"I know."

"The poor man."

"Kilmartin?"

"Maloney."

"Because he can't interest a woman that much younger than he is?"

"She's not all that younger."

"Well, just how old would you say she is?" she demanded.

"She's not much older than you are."

Melissa turned away in anger. She would have liked to beat her fists on Arne's broad chest. He was only saying these things to hurt her, to punish her for the imagined slight of going to the game with Brian, but why should his remarks sting her as they did? She did not have a crush on Martin Kilmartin. A proof of this was the fact that she had felt no sense of loss when she saw Martin succumbing to the flagrant flirtation of Deirdre Lacey. Her thoughts had gone immediately to Padraig Maloney. And without doubt she noticed his reaction whenever he saw the two together.

A beard is a mask, of course, and she had never seen his face unbearded. It was as if he had a single expression, no matter what. The eyes might give him away but they in turn were masked by the cloudy lenses of his glasses. But she knew how he felt and Melissa's heart went out to him. A man should not have to suffer so for someone like Deirdre.

Was it catty to say that there was nothing to Deirdre, no mind or soul, her undeniable beauty aside?

"She writes well," Maloney replied when she had obliquely suggested this to him.

"About other people's writing."

"So?"

"I mean she's not creative."

He lost interest in contradicting her. Did he think she was alluding to his own inability to write a poem? How different he was from Brian Elliot.

Going to the game with Brian had been a more exciting experience than Melissa would have believed. She hadn't the faintest idea what was going on out on the field but few of those in the student section seemed to pay close attention to the contest. Everyone stood throughout the game, sitting down was infra dig. A girl was handed up and down the rows, held high above the heads of those who passed her on. She squealed and writhed but made it safely to the top to earn a cheer. Some minutes later, Melissa noticed her walking down the steps. People acted drunk but there was no sign of drinking. The first time Brian offered his massive plastic drink holder, she shook her head. When later she did accept she almost choked.

"What is it?"

"Whiskey sours."

"You might have warned me."

Several times he fought his way down to where food was available and brought it back to her. He shook away her offer to come along.

Gallantry, it seemed. It was odd how she felt perfectly at ease among the heedless undergraduates.

Notre Dame won the game and the students went mad. The whole student section remained through all the postgame festivities, band saluting band, and then she and Brian were carried along in the mass movement as they descended. They were approaching an exit, when Brian took her arm and pulled her back.

"What's wrong?"

He turned toward her, eyes closed but smiling. When he opened them, he turned around.

"The coast is clear."

"Who was it?"

"My father. He would have insisted we go with him."

Melissa knew that Padraig Maloney had been asked to breakfast to meet Elliot senior, but doubted that he connected Brian with the rich alumnus. Was Brian rich? She supposed he was, or would be. The breakfast had something to do with a possible benefaction, but Maloney was vaguely indifferent to what it might be.

"I wish they'd leave us alone," he'd say.

"They" stood for administrators, deans and their assistants, provosts, vice-presidents, the hostile army employed to disturb the even tenor of the academic life. Padraig's complaints about the paperwork always led to a citation from Auden, the clerk who writes, "on a pink official form 'I do not like my work.' " Melissa usually did such work for him. He had a secretary of sorts, Mrs. Bumstead, chosen apparently for her name and not her skills, who whiled away her day surreptitiously reading romance novels, a headset clamped to her thinning hair, Muzak to accompany the torrid plots. Padraig always addressed her formally as Mrs. Bumstead, giving it an emphatically trochaic pronunciation, although her baptismal name Prudence was also tempting. Mrs. Bumstead confided to Melissa that the only reason she worked was to secure an eventual tuition reduction for her son. The son, Eric, wore massive tennis shoes and oversize trousers. His hair was artfully dyed a number of colors—yellow, blue, a dash of red—his expression mindless. Melissa doubted that Mrs. Bumstead would ever benefit from that tuition reduction. Maloney regarded Eric with bemusement.

"I think of Augustine, in North Africa, hearing of the hordes of barbarians descending from the north, occupying the empire, putting out the lights. Eric the red—and yellow and blue."

"Looks are deceiving," Melissa said.

"You really ought to write down such thoughts."

"Oh ha."

He put his big arm around her and tugged her against him. Melissa felt dizzy, his beard brushed her cheek before he let her go.

"I'm going to the game," she said.

"So am I."

"You are!"

"David Simmons sent me some tickets."

"Plural?"

"Two."

"Who will you take?" If he asked her to go with him she would desert Brian Elliot in a shot.

"I may change my mind and not go."

"You could make a fortune selling them."

"You too? Money, money, money."

After the game, Celtic Studies threw a party, a tradition on home game Saturdays.

When she asked Maloney if he had seen the game, he nodded. "It was on television. But I missed the end of it."

"You didn't go?"

"I never go."

"We won."

"We?"

"Notre Dame."

Maloney's snobbery about athletics and money was comic. Few faculty members admitted to being fans of the university's teams, although many were, perhaps a majority. But those professing disdain for the conjunction of sports and learning were more apt to be heard. With Padraig Maloney it seemed an acquired complaint, a language he had learned, not his native tongue. So why did he do it? You might just as well wonder why the only political viewpoint you heard expressed on campus was to the left of Lenin, the excessively well-paid faculty enjoying the radical chic of imagined solidarity with the oppressed. Jeans, open shirts, gray tweed sport jackets, and sneakers had become a uniform.

"Is your father a Republican?" she asked Brian.

"Of course."

"Of course!"

"He's very pro-life." He looked at her. "So am I."

"Good." She gripped his arm. She was pro-life too, wasn't she?

Sometimes Melissa felt like a lump of play dough that could be shaped by any dominant person. She would echo Padraig or Kilmartin and probably Brian too. But not Arne. He came and stood resentfully before her, a large plastic cup of beer in his hand.

"I thought you weren't interested in football," he said accusingly.

"It was the first game I've seen since I came here."

"Did you enjoy it?"

"Weren't you there?"

"I meant, how did you like it?"

She felt a perverse desire to say it had been awful, if only to baffle Arne. *Your honeyed appellation is sweet upon my ear.* Remembering the line made her feel sorry for him.

"It was fun."

"I was there too."

"In the student section?"

"Where else?"

Odd to think that he had been there in that anonymous mass of fans. Had his been one of the pair of hands that handed that girl upward?

When she got away to Padraig's side, she said, "How was breakfast with the president?"

He shrugged. "I think I was a disappointment."

"What is Mr. Elliot like?"

"From central casting."

It was *de rigueur* to be disdainful of potential benefactors. Once poets and scholars had patrons to whom they wrote fawning dedications. Now they kowtowed to impersonal foundations and the NEA without any sense that this was demeaning. Why should one strain at benefactors if he were willing to swallow obsequious grant proposals? Melissa had helped him fill out the forms. More paper.

At the party, Deirdre and Martin Kilmartin were the cynosure of every eye, a hymeneal couple wreathed in bashful smiles. Melissa tried to imagine the two in one another's arms and could not. It would have been pleasant to imagine Deirdre the dominating wife and Martin the doomed Robert Louis Stevenson, heading for an early death. But moribundity was part of Martin's charm.

"Did you know that Lady Anne Gregory once visited Notre Dame?" she asked Padraig.

"No!"

"Professor Roger Knight told me."

"I would need proof."

"I'll get it."

Her heart warmed at the thought of Roger Knight. Was that her fate, to be the doting younger woman to helpless middle-aged men?

Martin sneezed and the room fell silent. Once a sneeze had nearly undone him, as if his soul could be expelled in a gusty breath. He was put in a chair, Deirdre hovered, the moment passed. Could death come so easily? Martin held a handkerchief to his face and looked around with widened eyes. He still held a lighted cigarette in the pale fingers of one hand. He took away the handkerchief and then, as if he were performing a trick, put the cigarette to his mouth. He might have been taking hemlock.

11

THANKSGIVING CAME AND THE Knight brothers invited Father Carmody and Greg Whelan to share the massive turkey that Roger had prepared. It was served with all the traditional accompaniments—sweet potatoes, stuffing, cranberry sauce, pickles, olives and other assorted condiments, mashed potatoes and gravy from the bird—and everyone but Roger drinking deep of a Chilean red. Two kinds of pie, mince and pumpkin, were served with coffee afterward. It was a lovely day, bright and cold, yesterday's snow still fresh and sparkling in the sun. Phil had another feast of holiday football. All Notre Dame home games had been played, there remained a fateful contest with Air Force, the outcome of which would settle the post-season play, if any, of the Fighting Irish. Father Carmody and Phil argued long and earnestly about the method used to select teams for the great bowl games that started the new calendar year.

Melissa had gone to Midlothian, Michigan, with Brian Elliot for the holiday. Thoughts of the Elliot family prompted Roger to talk with Greg Whelan about the proposal David Simmons had recently made about an Elliott donation.

Simmons had come to Roger during the week after the Michigan game, his eyes alight, a Greek bearing gifts. He began with a paean of praise for James Elliot and his loyalty and devotion to Notre Dame.

"I know his son Brian."

"He mentioned that! That's good. Let me just lay out what I have been thinking before you react, okay?"

The generosity of James Elliot had been seeking an appropriate major outlet at the university and Simmons had been trying to come up with something fitting. He had suggested various things, none with much enthusiasm, but then he had an epiphany.

"Malachy O'Neill! If there is anyone who is at the center of Elliot's memories about Notre Dame it is O'Neill. Of course you will have heard of him. A problem with anyone whose influence has been exclusively in the classroom is that it is difficult to convey to someone who wasn't there what he was like. Well and good. But if we think of O'Neill as a symbol as well as a historical personage, possibilities beyond a shrine to the man occur. What we are thinking of is a Malachy O'Neill Center of Catholic Literature."

"You've already spoken with him about it?"

"Yes. And he is enthusiastic. Of course everything is still vague at this stage, but calling it a Center of Catholic Literature immediately brought you to mind. Because of your endowed chair? The center could simply be a setting for what you're already doing."

Simmons was thinking big. Not only would there be a separate building, it would have its own special library, and beside sponsoring conferences and inviting lecturers it would have resident fellows working on appropriate topics.

"What it would not be is another academic department. The obstacles to introducing a new instructional unit are formidable, there is a gamut of committees to be faced—the graduate council, the academic council, the provost's advisory committee. It would be the fourth millennium before the thing got underway. But a center is another kettle of fish entirely."

There were analogues of what Simmons was suggesting already in place on campus. It represented a new emphasis in academe, an effort to bring together different disciplines rather than to strengthen their differences.

Simmons spoke with the fervor of a man worried about being interrupted. He was very much in the grips of the idea and did not want Roger to react in any way at all right off.

"All I ask is that you think about it. That's all James Elliot asks at this point. I said he was enthusiastic. He is. He is not an excitable man. But he is excited about having Roger Knight as the director of the new center."

"I am acquainted with him, you know."

"Why do you think he's enthusiastic? Let me tell you a little story, strictly *entre nous*."

Simmons then related the tale of the breakfast he had arranged for Elliot and Padraig Maloney. "I had the idea that Celtic Studies might provide the connection. Wrong. From the word go, I saw it was a big mistake."

"Celtic Studies was expecting Elliot to . . ."

"No, no. Nothing was broached. The chemistry between Elliot and Maloney was so obviously wrong that all we did was eat breakfast. Nothing was proposed, nothing discussed. There would be no possible grounds for resentment."

Roger agreed to think about it. He tried to express his doubts, but Simmons cut him off. "Think about it. Talk with a few people confidentially, if you want. Give it serious thought."

At the door, he looked back at Roger.

"I cannot emphasize too much what this means to the university and to a valued alumnus."

To discuss such a project, however confidential the conversation was supposed to be, would inevitably introduce it into the campus pipeline. There are no secrets in the academic community. Administrators confide in others, perhaps in the half-conscious expectation that a trial balloon will be released. Committees sworn to professional secrecy regularly find that their proceedings are known and discussed far and wide. But then Roger saw no need to discuss the idea.

Philip would be all for anything that consolidated their position at Notre Dame. For Roger to be not only an endowed professor but director of a center whose agenda he could set and implement would not seem to Phil an offer Roger could reasonably refuse. But on an impulse he trusted he mentioned it now to Greg Whelan.

"I can't believe he's serious, Greg."

"Of course he's serious."

"The money was originally destined for Celtic Studies." Melissa too had mentioned Maloney's breakfast with the fat cat alumnus, and the expectations among those in Celtic Studies was that a huge financial boost was in the offing.

"The donor has to be the judge of that. There is a lot to be said for a Malachy O'Neill Center."

"Tell me everything you know about Malachy O'Neill."

"But you already know about him."

Roger displayed a pudgy palm. "Pretend that I have never heard of him before. Start from the beginning."

The assistant archivist was silent for a moment as he marshaled the formidable information he had amassed over the years as he pored over the holdings of the archives. And then he began.

It is the rare person who can speak impromptu with the orderliness and pith of Greg Whelan's portrait of Malachy O'Neill. His performance was all the more remarkable because of his speech impediment, although this never bothered him when he talked with Roger. By and large, Greg's interlocutors would imagine that his thought processes were as staccato as his speech. That this was far from being the case was once more clear.

Greg began by evoking the Notre Dame of several decades ago, inviting Roger to think away half the buildings on campus, remove women students from the picture, and imagine a community of some seven thousand male residents, few permitted to have automobiles, whose life was bounded by the campus, especially in the winter months. Computers did not exist although there was a computing center, harbinger of the future but not yet a household word: there were no computer clusters scattered across campus where students spent untold hours. Then, O'Shaughnessy Hall was *the* classroom building although there were also some rooms in the Main Building assigned to the Arts College. The bookstore was a place where textbooks for courses and little else could be purchased. On its erstwhile site now stood an equivocal building devoted to this and that.

This was a sketch of the Notre Dame in which O'Neill had flourished as a teacher. But what of the Notre Dame O'Neill had known as a student in the years just after World War II? An all-male school, of course, enrollment between four and five thousand. Proportionately fewer residence halls. Student automobiles not permitted and the young men even more campus bound, their lives defined by what they did as students. There was no competition from television, students were not permitted to have radios in their rooms; the lights were turned off in the halls at an early hour, the master switch thrown by the rector, almost invariably a priest of the Congregation of Holy Cross.

And Greg suggested another way in which early stages of the school could be imaginatively reconstructed.

"Go to the community cemetery and see how many graves date from 1945. Most of them. It is in the few rows that precede them that you will find the priests who influenced Malachy O'Neill as a student."

The note that Greg stressed as definitive of O'Neill's outlook was the superiority of Catholic culture.

"He saw Notre Dame as in the mainstream, vitally connected with the great cultural events of western civilization. A liberal arts education aimed at introducing students to the great achievements of Christendom in philosophy, theology, art, architecture music, literature. These were not the achievement let alone the possession of WASPs, Roger. These were Catholic!"

The courses Malachy O'Neill had taken as a student and the courses he gave as a professor were not considered to be specialized courses, Catholic writers as opposed to others, a small and sectarian group out of the mainstream.

"O'Neill insisted that it was secular American higher education that was out of the mainstream. A kind of proof of this was the revival of liberal arts at Columbia, Chicago, and St. John's, during the thirties."

Mortimer Adler and Robert Hutchins looked to the Catholic colleges for the continuation of what they wanted to recover.

"Now it has to be recovered here," Greg concluded. "I suppose that is the point of the proposed center."

Roger Knight doubted that David Simmons or James Elliot would have been capable of stating the rationale for the center as ably as Greg Whelan had.

"How did we lose it? That is another and longer story."

Greg supplied Roger with photocopies of Malachy O'Neill materials from the archives. It turned out that the man had written a few things after all. There was an essay or two in the literary magazine of which he had been faculty moderator. There were contributions to *The Scholastic* when he was a student. Over the next several weeks, Roger kept Simmons at bay while he tried to enter into the mind-set of Malachy O'Neill.

"I got a call from James Elliot," Phil said in early December.

"How is he?"

"He wants to know when you're going to decide."

There was pressure from Simmons as well. Finally Roger set a deadline.

"Early January. I want to have the break between semesters to think about it."

12 "A MAN NAMED WEBER WAS asking about you," Greg Whelan said to Roger Knight.

"Weber."

"Donald Weber."

The friend—or was it enemy?—of James Elliot whose claim to have been in the classroom on the day that Malachy O'Neill fell to the floor dead had turned out to be true, much to Elliot's chagrin. Roger remembered Weber's somewhat hostile reaction to his own appointment as Huneker professor. And then Melissa came by to tell him that a Professor Weber from Midlothian had been talking with Padraig Maloney.

"Well, Midlothian is Celtic enough."

"You know him?"

"Weber? Yes, we've met."

"Well, you didn't make another fan."

"Another?"

Melissa actually blushed.

Roger was told by Becky Fontana in English that Weber had dropped in there in the role of successful alumnus of the program.

"I suppose he talked about Malachy O'Neill?"

"He had all kinds of anecdotes that some found funny."

"You didn't?"

Becky was in her mid-fifties and had huge, wide-spaced blue eyes that seemed never to blink. She wrote enigmatic short stories that had yet to find a publisher and had been writing a study of Carson McCullers for years. Her eyes grew if possible larger.

"Of course my colleagues regard anyone who taught here prior to their own arrival as by definition incompetent. The legend of Malachy O'Neill is an obligatory object of derision. Weber corroborated all their fondest prejudices."

"That is odd. He once told me that O'Neill was the major formative influence in his life."

"He talked about you too. Did you have lunch with him and the trash king of Michigan recently?"

"With my brother Phil."

"Roger, you do realize that there are those who resent your position here, don't you?"

"Seated?"

"Not that it matters, of course. Weber was assured what a joke your appointment is considered to be. A sort of quid pro quo for his stories about Malachy O'Neill."

"Well, well."

Phil ran into Weber in the bar of the Morris Inn, where the visiting professor had apparently been for some time before Phil's arrival.

"And how's your enormous brother?" Weber sputtered, looking about as if for an appreciative audience. But there was only a mustachioed man beside him at the bar, holding his drink with both hands.

Phil said that Roger was fine. "Flourishing."

"Is that right? I'm glad to hear it."

"I suppose you've visited Malachy O'Neill's grave."

"Ha!" And Weber's eyes darted to the man beside him.

"Have you heard of Jim Elliot's proposal for a Malachy O'Neill Center of Catholic Literature?"

The little man with Weber exploded, sputtering his drink in several directions, and launched a tirade against the influence of donors on the direction of the university.

"He's even picked the director he wants!" the little man cried.

Weber stood back as his companion vented his wrath. He seemed to be a member of the faculty. His name was Sauer and he taught English. "I am, for my sins, the Malachy O'Neill professor of literature." He went on from the proposed center to the travesty of Celtic Studies.

"A haven for bogus bards."

Weber snickered.

"Do you know there is a course being offered on the Celtic Twilight by someone who has never written a word on the subject? We're being taken over by amateurs."

"Isn't that your brother's course?" Weber asked.

Sauer stared. "Is Roger Knight your brother?"

"He is."

"Do you have a faculty appointment too?" Sauer smiled evilly.

"No, I'm gainfully employed."

Phil left. He was still surprised by the pettiness some academics were capable of, but he did not trust himself to be patient with these two, particularly when it was an implicit attack on Roger.

"Sauer?" Roger said. "He's the author of the hatchet job on Martin Kilmartin in *The Scholastic.* 'Irish Bards and Scotch Consumers.' His main complaint is that Kilmartin has learned nothing from Pound."

The following day Weber tapped on the door of Roger's office in Earth Sciences. Roger's window overlooked the parking lot and, beyond, the grotto and lake.

"Busy?"

"Come in, come in. I heard you were on campus."

"I ran into your brother. That's why I'm here."

Weber sat and looked around, doing a 180-degree turn. "Not very posh, is it?"

"I like it. And it's convenient. Getting in and out of. I leave my cart right outside."

"Did your brother tell you of Sauer's drunken remarks?"

"I gather he doesn't share your admiration for Malachy O'Neill."

"He never knew him! All these Johnny-come-latelys on the faculty can't accept the fact that giants once walked this campus."

"Your friend Elliot wants a center to be named after O'Neill."

"A great idea! And Jim has the money to do it."

Weber continued to take in Roger's office.

"I can't get over what a dump they've put you in. My office at Midlothian is sumptuous compared to this."

"I would not want anything sumptuous."

"You will have one, though, when you take over the center."

Roger tried to laugh it off, but Weber was relentless.

"You've been offered it, haven't you?"

"Can you see me as administrator?"

"How could you turn it down?"

"By thinking of more worthy nominees."

"Who?"

"Martin Kilmartin." Roger spoke the name as one drawn out of a hat, but once uttered it seemed right to him. He told Weber how accomplished a poet Kilmartin was.

Weber was staring at him. He found his voice.

"I understand he is consumptive."

"He's certainly not robust. I believe the problem is his heart. He is so fragile he could kill himself with a sneeze."

"Literally?"

"I am quoting him."

"What do you think of his poetry?"

"I was just going to put that question to you."

Weber threw back his head and closed his eyes. "His is the purest lyric voice since Edna St. Vincent Millay." His eyes opened. "She is my favorite American poet."

"And you rank Kilmartin with her?"

"Emphatically. And you say he could die at any moment?"

"Something true of you and me."

"You're a philosopher."

"My degree is in philosophy. But I don't need a degree to know that all men are mortal."

Weber adopted a serious expression and nodded. Then, after another look around: "Does Jim Elliot know the kind of office you have?"

"Professor Weber, please. I could not be more content than I am."

A pause. "I believe you."

It was a statement Roger would not have been able to make of Weber.

After Weber was gone, Roger pondered the remarkably conflicting impressions the man made. From his manner, one would have taken Weber to be a dear friend of Roger's, happy with his good fortune, miffed that he did not have a more impressive office. But if Melissa and Becky Fontana had heard correctly, Weber was resentful of Roger and of Martin Kilmartin as well. And of course Roger remembered Weber's incredulous reaction to his Notre Dame appointment when they had first met last summer in Midlothian.

13 BRIAN WAS NOW KNOWN AS "the son of the benefactor," at least to Padraig Maloney, a taunting title, reminiscent of the phrase with which he had once jolted a class awake. "Joyce was a son of an habitual drinker." Addressing a classroom of no longer somnolent undergraduates, Maloney went on to discuss Joyce's linguistic jokes. "Son of a benefactor" was disguised invective, Brian knew it. Did Maloney think he had anything to do with his father's decision not to lavish money on Celtic Studies? He asked Melissa.

"Of course he doesn't." She worked her lips. "But others have heard of the breakfast. Couldn't you talk to him?"

"Maloney?"

"Your father!"

His cover had been blown by his father's decision not to give money to Celtic Studies. A student with the same name as a building was unlikely to be suspected of a blood relationship to a donor. His father had always been discreet in his generosity, all but anonymous, so Brian's time at Notre Dame had been like that of any other student who came from an affluent home. Such things did not matter on campus. Everyone dressed alike, the residences were great levelers, only a car might give a clue, and Brian had a SUV whose like could be found by the dozens in the student parking lots. His family was very big in the small pond of Midlothian, but even there the source of the Elliot wealth was the object of half-hidden snickers. One of the attractions of medicine was the esteem in which doctors were held for what they did.

"Talking with my father wouldn't do any good."

"What does he have against Celtic Studies?"

What did she imagine the attraction of the program might be for a potential benefactor of the university? It could be a hundred times better than it was and it wouldn't matter. Nothing and no one could compete in his father's mind with an opportunity to immortalize Malachy O'Neill. Brian had got a version of the proposed center from his father.

"Now if Roger Knight will agree . . ." His father's voice trailed wistfully away.

Brian was sure that Roger Knight's delay was artless, but he could not have hit on a more effective way to make James Elliot determined that he should be the first director of the Malachy O'Neill Center of Catholic Literature.

"The first director. A couple of years, to get it started, that's all it would take." His father paused. "Has he ever mentioned it to you?"

"No."

"If it ever should come up, tell him how much it would mean to Notre Dame."

Brian gave his father credit for not wanting to plaster the family name around the campus. Better to honor faculty than donors. Brian avoided like sin bringing up the matter with Roger Knight. It was Roger who startled him one day by asking what he knew of Malachy O'Neill.

"My father has mentioned him."

"Of course he would have. I am looking for the average undergraduate's reaction to the name. I wonder if it would even be recognized?"

"Probably not."

"He really was an interesting man."

Roger Knight had apparently made a study of O'Neill, gleaning from the materials in the archives and some published memoirs of students what could be learned of a man who had left so meager a trail. It was a moment when Brian could have urged Roger Knight to take the post offered him. He was deterred by Philip Knight's mention of David Simmons.

"You'd think he was trying to sell Roger a car," the private investigator said with disgust.

"It's his job, Phil," Roger said.

"Selling cars?"

Greg Whelan had stepped up his own campaign to get Roger to accept the directorship of the new center. A new development was that the university had just come into possession of more papers of Malachy O'Neill which his sister had preserved in the family home, holding them back when the first gift was made.

"You have to go with me to make an inventory, Roger."

"That I will certainly do."

"Did you tell Arne I went home with you for Thanksgiving?"

"No. Is it a secret?"

Melissa had asked Brian the question in an odd tone he could not interpret. Was she indignant? And with whom, him or Arne—or herself? Midlothian had been in the blah period between the disappearance of the leaves of autumn and the cosmetic snow that could turn the platted town on its flat plain into a pretty sight. Not that he apologized for his hometown. Brian hadn't been quite sure himself about the wisdom of asking Melissa home for Thanksgiving. He had asked her in the certainty that she would turn him down. It was one thing to be with her on campus and quite another to introduce her to his mother and father and siblings in Midlothian. He could see that they were sizing her up as a permanent addition, and how could he blame them? She and his father got along terrifically, talking about Irish authors, and Melissa proved to be adept in the kitchen, mixing with the other women easily. But the thought that he had brought home a future bride filled Brian with terror.

"Arne said something?"

"He doesn't have to say it."

"I'll talk to him."

"About what?"

"I should have asked him for Thanksgiving too. I'll tell him that."

Melissa ran a finger along her upper lip. "Are you serious?"

"About talking to him."

"That you would have asked him?"

"Why not?"

Half a minute silence. "I wish you had."

When he left her he felt that he had broken an engagement. My God, he felt free! The thought of being tied down to Melissa, or any other girl, just now was oppressive. He had to get back to playing the field.

"Three's a crowd," Arne said, when Brian told him he wished he'd been with them in Midlothian for Thanksgiving.

"Three! We had a house full."

Arne's wary look began to fade. They had been friends, but Melissa had come between them. Brian punched the big Scandihoovian on the arm. "You can take her home at Christmas."

Arne brushed away the punch. "I've got your permission, have I?"

"How's the poetry going?"

It was a dig. But he could see in Arne's eyes the thought that he and Melissa had whooped it up in Midlothian talking about Arne Jensen writing poetry.

"Stick it in your ear." Arne's answering punch was not quite playful.

(14)   UNDER THE IMPETUS OF JAMES
Elliot's proposed center and Roger Knight's interest in O'Neill, Greg Whelan had reviewed all the primary and collateral materials in the archives. And so he came to the effects of the late Louise O'Neill. The boxes that had been sent to the Notre Dame archives ten years before by the sister of the famous bachelor don had been duly cataloged by some nameless predecessor, but Greg Whelan had never before perused them personally. The bulk of the trove consisted of letters to his sister from Malachy, which while composed on the typewriter exhibited a personalized overcoming of the mechanical in a manner reminiscent of the letters of Ezra Pound.

Like her brother, Louise had never married, and equally like him she had devoted herself to teaching. In her case, a Catholic girls academy in a western suburb of Chicago. She had lived in the house in which she and Malachy had been raised, a house which—as Greg had learned to his surprise—she had bequeathed to Notre Dame in her will.

"What happened to it?" Roger asked.

"I was hoping you could put the question to Father Carmody."

"Of course."

The old priest lifted his brows and cocked his head at the question. They were at table in the Knight apartment, Roger and Phil, Greg Whelan, and Father Carmody. If anyone might be called a living archive of Notre Dame's past, it would be Father Carmody. As a young man, before his hair turned first gray, then white, he had been known as the Éminence Rouge of successive university administrations. He had not served as president or vice-president, nor had he ever been religious superior of the priests of the congregation. His name did not appear in routine accounts of the university's past. During his active years, there had been no need to affix a title to his role. It was informal, in any case. His counsel and discretion, his practical wisdom, were at the disposal of anyone involved in directing the university. He was a man devoid of personal ambition and vanity—those virtues, and vices as they sometimes become, he reserved for the glory of Notre Dame. He was jealous of her reputation, both athletic and academic. He had known and admired Malachy O'Neill, however much he had lamented his weakness in the matter of alcohol, and his pulse quickened at the prospect opened up by James Elliot's proposal.

"Yes, yes, of course. I had forgotten about the house."

"Does the university still own it?"

A frown formed on the priest's brow. "You wouldn't think it possible that we should sell something like that, would you?"

This was as close as he would come to criticize administrators of recent years who had been less ready to call upon his advice and whose judgments he sometimes, if discreetly, deplored. With Roger and his brother, the priest had been frank about developments he did not like, but he was unlikely to say anything with Greg Whelan at the table.

"Let me check on it."

He did not mean tomorrow. When they rose from table, he asked to use the telephone and Roger took him into his study. "Devereux will know," the priest said as Roger closed the door on him.

Maurice Devereux, an old companion in arms of Father Carmody's, legal counsel to the university for decades, had the information at his fingertips. Father Carmody's memory had not betrayed him. The house had indeed been sold.

"What point would there be in the university's owning suburban Chicago real estate?" Father Carmody said, as if repeating an excuse he could not himself accept. Was he perhaps thinking that the boyhood home of Malachy O'Neill might have been moved to campus to house the proposed new center?

That might very well have been that. But the following day, Maurice Devereux remembered something else. The house had been purchased by a Notre Dame alumnus motivated by fond memories of Malachy O'Neill. Attempts to get in touch with him brought the sad news of his recent death. The house, it emerged, was once more on the market. Father Carmody put through a call to Midlothian, Michigan.

There was no need to persuade James Elliot of the desirability of buying the house in which Malachy O'Neill had passed his childhood. It was that house to which O'Neill had gone whenever he absented himself from Notre Dame, so that the association had been continuous.

"I will buy it on behalf of the university," James Elliot said.

"That might not be wise," Father Carmody replied.

"Why not?"

"We owned it once and sold it."

James Elliot reaction was that of a youth who has been told the facts of life in too gruff a manner. On second thought, as a precaution, he would buy it in his own name and give it to the university with the proviso that in the event of any future sale he would have the right of first refusal.

To these negotiations Greg Whelan was privy, whether directly or indirectly, and when the house had been bought it was he who was sent on behalf of the university to inspect its newly recovered property. Roger and Phil went along, driving over in their converted van.

Cottonwood Ridge did not have the éclat of Oak Park nor its claim on the tourist's attention. But until the mid December trip to the suburb, there was no reason to believe that a writer of rare ability, and accomplishment, had grown up in Cottonwood Ridge. The interstates and other roads engineered to facilitate the daily filling and emptying of the Loop had not been kind to Cottonwood Ridge. Its one-time Main Street was now a six-lane speedway which divided what had once been a unified town. The side on which the O'Neill home was located had become the commercial half of the suburb, with the usual ruinous effects. But miraculously the house itself and its immediate neighborhood had retained the simple dignity of yore.

A great brick house, three floors high, and above the third floor little dormer windows marking the attic. The front veranda was as wide as the house and was marked with thick pillars. The windows on either side of the main entrance were leaded. Phil unlocked the door. There was a moment of hesitation. Who should enter first? It was decided that Greg was there on official university business, so he preceded them into the house.

Once inside they made the delighted discovery that the previous owner had bought the house in order to preserve it just as it was. A cleaning service visited fortnightly so that the furnishings in which Malachy had been raised and his sister dwelt throughout her life were not only unchanged but in superb repair. The trio moved reverently through the rooms, mounted to the second floor and found Malachy's room. Two bookcases against the wall, containing among other things the complete works of Francis Finn, S. J. *"Tom Playfair,"* Greg said reverently, leafing through a volume. *"Percy Wynn,"* said Roger, leafing through another. On the wall hung O'Neill's Notre Dame diploma. There was a photograph of the Grotto. There was a rosary hanging from the bedpost.

Roger let Greg and Phil look into the attic while he sat on O'Neill's bed. But within minutes he was startled to his feet by a great shout above. He hurried down the hallway to the door that opened on the attic stairway.

Greg Whelan stood at the top of the attic stairway, holding a loose-leaf notebook in his hand.

"Stories," he cried. "By Malachy O'Neill."

Huffing and puffing, Roger climbed into the airless attic.

It would be overly dramatic to compare the next hours to entry into the treasures of a pyramid. The attic was filled with mementos and impedimenta that the O'Neill family had accumulated over the years. But neatness was all. Louise's things were kept separately— her certificate of confirmation, her high school diploma, a plaque conferred on her after her first twenty-five years of teaching. And photograph albums! Two were of special interest. They were filled with snapshots marking the stages of the life of Malachy O'Neill. But it was in the boxes containing the childhood effects of Malachy that the real treasures were found. The first fruit of the search there was a notebook containing half a dozen stories from the pen of Malachy O'Neill. Literally from his pen, written in the graceful hand familiar to Greg Whelan from documents in the archives.

The three men emptied the attic of Malachy O'Neill memorabilia and put the boxes in the van for the trip back to Notre Dame.

On Wednesday of that week Greg hit what he described as real pay dirt. Typewritten, bound, apparently only privately circulated, if that, was *The Ballad of Pearl Harbor* by Malachy O'Neill.

15   "IT'S BAD CHESTERTON," MAR-
tin Kilmartin observed when Melissa asked
what he thought of the recently discovered ballad by Malachy O'Neill.
He added, "At best."

Do poets ever praise one another? Of course they do, when there
is no question of competition or comparison. A critic might praise a
poet—Padraig had said fulsome things about Kilmartin's verse—and
vice versa, though this could risk the charge of opportunism.

"Do you like Chesterton?"

"Not really."

"The Ballad of the White Horse."

To Melissa's surprise, Kilmartin rattled off a stanza

> *People, if you have any prayers,*
> *Say prayers for me:*
> *And lay me under a Christian stone*
> *In that lost land I thought my own,*
> *To wait till the holy horn is blown*
> *And all poor men are free.*

"Not bad," Kilmartin conceded. "But to keep that up for a hundred
pages and more? Dense pages? The world has outlived poetry by the
yard."

The Wasteland? Pound's *Cantos?* But there was no point in ar-
guing. Such judgments were expressions of likes and dislikes, not
truths about the object spoken of.

"He was wise to bury it," Padraig said. "It makes him a better critic than poet."

"I like it," Arne said, and he lifted his chin as he spoke.

"So do I," Melissa said.

"You do?" Arne lowered his chin and smiled. What a nice smile he had. "That's the kind of poetry I'd like to write. Not Kilmartin stuff."

The poet had returned to Arne's single line in class in a discussion on the need to be able to recognize the bad and awful in verse. Melissa could almost hear Arne's teeth grinding. His liking for Malachy O'Neill's ballad could be a simple reaction to the really cruel remarks Kilmartin had made.

"Have you been talking with him, Arne?"

"You don't talk, you listen."

Roger Knight had been given a photocopy of the bound typescript now in the archives and had read it several times.

"So what do you think?" Melissa asked.

"It's not clear that it was written when he was young. Of course the attack on Pearl Harbor would have been a traumatic event of his childhood."

"What difference does it make when it was written?"

"None. Look at Keats."

"But you don't think he was a Keats?"

"Oh no. Melissa, it is an interesting effort. To have written so much so tolerably well is beyond the powers of ninety-nine percent of us. But it was an effort. Listen:

> Once they were called the Sandwich Isles
> Boasting a king and queen
> Positioned precisely in between
> East and West by identical miles,
> They drew the world's merchant marine.

"I heard there was a plan to publish it."

"It deserves publication, I think. As the work of a legendary Notre Dame figure. Did you know that both Churchill and Eisenhower painted? Fairly well too, by all accounts. But if someone bought a painting by one of them, his motives would not be simply artistic, would they?"

"It sounds like you've decided not to accept the directorship of the new center."

"Does it? That's not true. I am still pondering it."

"I wish you'd take it."

"I wish I could find someone who wished I wouldn't."

"Come on over to Celtic Studies."

"Oh?"

"They have developed the myth that you jobbed them out of money meant for them."

"I have to disabuse them of such thoughts."

"Good luck."

16 THERE WAS A DELIVERY EN-
trance on the west side of Flanner Hall and a
parking area from which the snow had been cleared where Roger was
able to park his golf cart out of the weather and close to the doorway.
Several people huddled outside in the cold, smoking, their expressions those once seen on the denizens of Asian opium dens when a
western camera pushed its prurient lens into iniquity. Chesterton had
remarked that Americans had turned two of God's blessings, alcohol
and tobacco, into vices. If only we hadn't turned vices into virtues
at the same time.

As Roger rose in the elevator, he was not thinking of what he
would say to Padraig Maloney. His appointment with him was half
an hour off. Meanwhile, he wanted to drop in on Martin Kilmartin.
The poet had sounded surprised when Roger identified himself.

Kilmartin said, "When we first met I had no idea who you were.
I let you talk about my poetry when we could have discussed Baron
Corvo! Melissa should have described you better."

"You know Corvo?"

"Is the pope Polish? And I don't mean Hadrian VII."

Roger fitted himself carefully into the chair Kilmartin offered. "My
reputation is largely local. Like Malachy O'Neill's."

"Ah yes. I have been reading about the great discovery."

"The ballad? I prefer the shorter things. He was trying too hard,
I think, when he undertook the ballad."

"It's the only thing of his I've heard of."

"Perhaps you would like copies of some other things."

Kilmartin watched as Roger placed on the desk a manila envelope he had taken from his shoulder bag. "Photocopies. You needn't return them."

"I look forward to reading them," Kilmartin said carefully. "I hope I like them better than the ballad."

"I am here on quite another matter and I would like your advice."

"Yes?"

"I'm told that Professor Maloney thinks that I was instrumental in diverting money away from Celtic Studies. From a benefactor named Elliot."

"Were you?"

"No."

"So why would Maloney think so?"

"I shall shortly ask him that. I have an appointment with him in a few minutes. Naturally I do not like to be thought capable of such tricks."

"Do you think Maloney ever had a chance of getting money from Elliot?"

"I don't know."

"My theory is that Maloney blew it. And he needs you to blame his failure on."

Kilmartin seemed more amused than miffed by the thought that the program in which he taught was not going to have largesse rained upon it. But then it was unclear that he saw his presence at Notre Dame as more than a brief sojourn. Long-term thoughts would thus be uninteresting to him.

Padraig Maloney was anything but philosophical about the loss of the Elliot benefaction.

"It was a done deal! I had breakfast with the man, the president came and gave his blessing. So what happened?"

"What were you told happened?"

"That he changed his mind." Maloney sat forward and worked his beard. "Your brother attended the game with him and then he had supper at your place. After which he tells the foundation man it's all off. He wants to give the money to you for a mausoleum for some long-ago faculty member."

"I haven't accepted the offer to direct a center named after Malachy O'Neill."

"Holding out for an even better deal than they've offered?"

Roger laughed. "I lack all these Machiavellian virtues, Maloney. I will say this. Rather than have it thought that I influenced Elliot to change his mind and take up the idea of a center, I would refuse to be its director."

"What do you want from me, absolution?"

What *had* he expected? It is always difficult to see oneself as others do, and Roger was unable to see himself as one who would take advantage of his acquaintance with James Elliot to persuade him to give money where he neither wanted nor intended to give it. He found Padraig Maloney irksome, devoid of any collegial feeling. They spoke at cross-purposes for ten more minutes and then Roger was in the elevator, descending to his golf cart, anxious to get away. It had been a mistake to come.

Outside, snow flurries had begun. He pulled his cap tightly over his head, raised the collar of his coat, and headed into whiteness. Had he promised not to accept the directorship of the proposed Center for Catholic Literature? He could not think so, given Maloney's sarcastic reaction to his offer to do so. But he remained unsure whether he would accede to James Elliot's wishes.

17   BEFORE THE ADVENT OF KIL-
martin, Deirdre Lacey had been if not exactly
Padraig Maloney's girl, at least his constant and assumed companion.
Their easy mutual jocularity might have been a warning that whatever
seriousness was invested in the pact came entirely from his side.
Why could he not make poetry out of the anguish he felt at losing
her to Kilmartin? A possible line began and then unaccountably
stopped. "Ah love, let us be false to one another . . ." Bah. Unre-
quited love was the traditional nurturing ground of verse, but his
tears fell on barren ground. There was no gain from his loss. And
now there was the devoted Melissa, too young by far, too uncritically
adulatory, seemingly infatuated with him. He felt a duty to tell her
that he was not worth her interest. At the most recent departmental
party they had ended up side by side on a couch, he talking, she
listening. He hated the sound of his own voice when he pontificated
to her. But he felt avuncular, if not paternal. To lay a hand on her
would have been too much like violating his own young sister.

"Deirdre is so beautiful," Melissa said. Did she realize her words
were like a knife in his side?

"Ah yes."

Great ropes of tawny hair lay plaited on Deirdre's shoulders; she
wore a black dress of ankle length and a necklace of green stones.
Maloney could imagine saying a rosary on them, the sorrowful mysteries. But Deirdre doubtless saw herself as the Pietà, the dying or
dead poet in her arms, herself the object of hyperdulia. The best
analogy of her infatuation was the fatal attraction men condemned to
death had for women. Female defense lawyers fell in love with the

monsters they represented, sometimes married them. The moribund Kilmartin whose life might be sneezed away in a moment was irresistible to Deirdre. Was he the only one who saw her abject devotion, the glint of self-sacrifice in her eye? Martin's frail body and translucent face lit up by the great green eyes that drank in the world and transmuted it into lyrical effusions was a powerful aphrodisiac. A recent sonnet could only have been written with Deirdre in mind, but like her the poet expressed his love obliquely. There was something fated in their togetherness as if it had not been a matter of choice, but simply there to be recognized, and once recognized hidden by a mask of indifference.

The moment toward which the evening led was Kilmartin reading. He read Yeats's "The Choice" and then something of his own inspired by it.

> *Raging in the dark is what we do in sunlit*
> *hours, no need to wait till we are late*
> *and wispy howls among the monuments;*
> *our heavenly mansion to all intents*
> *unchosen, we will our will to spite.*

"So gloomy," Deirdre murmured.

"Just Irish."

But she was right, the level of melancholy in his verse rose as happiness threatened in the form of Deirdre. He was a great Catholic, Kilmartin, as devout as a widow, slipping off to Mass at Sacred Heart on weekdays, 12:15 in the crypt, with Orestes Brownson under stone in the main aisle, secretaries and other lower orders from the Main Building scattered here and there in the pews. Maloney had looked in once or twice, spying, following Kilmartin when he left Flanner, fearing he had a rendezvous with Deirdre, but all it was was Mass.

"What's wrong with him?" Melissa asked.

"Heart."

This puzzled her. Perhaps she thought he was speaking metaphorically. Maloney didn't understand it himself medically, it was some malformation that was life threatening, so Martin would doubtless live to be a hundred.

"Can't they operate?"

"Apparently not."

It was understood that he could go at any moment and sometimes Maloney prayed he would, making Deirdre a kind of widow and eligible again. He assumed Kilmartin would not marry, the demands of the nuptial couch a danger to his heart. How wrong he was. Last night at the party, Kilmartin coughed for attention and told the others their joyful news.

"Deirdre has consented to become my wife," he said, taking her hand, and drawing her to her feet beside him.

"Martin!" she cried. "You said it would be a secret."

Her eyes had darted to Maloney who had once explained to her the impossibility of Kilmartin's marrying, the information given at a time when she could not have imagined it to be self-serving. There had been no need to go on about it, Martin had such a valedictory air about him, the male counterpart of Camille on her couch, saying a long farewell to the world. Had Deirdre just noticed what she called gloominess in his poetry? Of course there were the light things. "Man is a National Animal." "Witless in Ringsend." Scarcely more than jingles. The serous ones dealt with the apparently inconsequential. "Old Shoes." "Pocket Lint." "Geography of My Window Shade."

Last night, with the hypocrisy of good manners, Maloney had jumped to his feet to congratulate the prospective bride and groom.

"And when and where will the great day be?"

"First Deirdre must visit Dublin. We will go when the semester ends."

18 DEIRDRE LACEY'S CONDO IN Shamrock Residences was rented in her own name and thus represented a new departure in her life, a first step toward the recovery of the freedom she had madly cast away out of infatuation for Fritz Davis, her husband of sorts, as she had belatedly explained to Martin Kilmartin after he had announced their engagement at the party.

"You're already married?"

"It was only a civil marriage."

"Only? I should think a civil marriage is the best kind." But he obviously could not joke it away.

"We were married by a judge in the courthouse."

How could she conjure up for him the tawdry scene in the small Minnesota town, the courthouse rising like a fist from the khaki lawn, baking in the August sun? The clerk from whom they bought the marriage licence sniffled and sneezed as he served them, checking the form Fritz had filled out. Deirdre stood beside him at the counter, not as high as his muscular shoulders, leaning against him as if his presence could negate the circumstances. She was nineteen, Fritz was twenty-five, both were high on crack, a delight to which he had introduced her three days before when she met him on the midway of the country fair. With his ponytail and roguish bandana he had seemed to her all that the wider world contained of excitement and fun. She was seduced on the first night, something she inferred the following morning, having no unclouded memory of her own deflowering. The motel room in which they misbehaved until the fateful trip to the courthouse seemed impossibly luxurious to her. They had pizza sent in and drugs were supplemented with beer. They honeymooned in Baraboo, Wisconsin, driving there on his Harley Davidson, Deirdre clinging to his back in terror and excitement.

"What do you do?"

"I'm on disability."

He had been injured in the army in a manner that was judged service-related. His reward was a pittance, but it was for life, and he had organized his life around his income. Their footloose wandering continued for months, biking from town to town, getting zonked in one motel after another, growing bored with one another.

"Why don't we stay here? I'll get a job."

"What for?"

"For something to do."

"Don't nag."

In moments of clarity she told herself she should take money from his wallet and board a bus for home. Instead she deserted him in Madison and took a job as a waitress near the university campus. Listening to the student chatter stirred memories of school and of how well she had done in her studies. Her high school sent a transcript of her grades without incident and she enrolled at the University of Wisconsin, taking courses indiscriminately, an intellectual orgy to match the one she had shared with Fritz. Fritz. From time to time her heart ached with memories of their months together. But it was not until she had earned her degree and began following graduate courses that he reappeared.

The sound of a motorcycle had always filled her with mixed emotions, fear that he would find her and beat her, a twisted hope that he would pull her up behind him and roar off with his captive. But five years passed and no motorcycle proved to be his. It was at the restaurant where she still waited tables that he found her.

"Remember me?"

"Fritz!"

There was a girl with him, windblown, tan, vacant-eyed. Deirdre looked at what she herself might have become.

"This is Molly."

"What can I bring you?"

She wanted to get to the kitchen and escape out the back way. In the flesh, Fritz was menacing and his smile satanic. How had she ever allowed herself to run off with this animal? She took their order, walked right through the kitchen and outside. She would explain later.

For days she kept to her room. To stay in Madison was to run the risk of his finding her. It never occurred to her that he would be as willing to forget her as she was to forget him.

She made her way eventually to South Bend, where she waited on tables until she was successful getting a secretarial job at Notre Dame, her knack with computers being the Open Sesame. The interview with Padraig Maloney had gone very well. She came upon him baffled by the unwillingness of his computer to respond to his wishes. She solved the problem. She got the job. Eventually she was given status as a special student so she could audit courses.

That had been two years ago, though it seemed mere months, but what a transforming time it had been. She was the person she claimed to be, fashioned for purposes of this new setting where at last she could truly flourish. She was in the academic world but not of it, privy to all the activities of a department yet independent of them. What she had never dreamt of was meeting someone like Martin Kilmartin.

Fritz had been rough and crude; Martin was fragile and refined. Fritz was an animal; Martin was an angel—at least at first. She had marveled at his language and the fact that he refined some of it into poetry represented merely a difference of degree not kind. The literal world receded and, with Martin, Deirdre entered the world of imagination. He was prophet and seer, one through whom spoke powers beyond his own. When he first took her in his arms she felt that she was being divinized by his touch.

Of course he was a male, there was little doubt of that, and she would not have wanted it otherwise. The ephemeral can take one only so far. Perhaps she had led him on, wanting to discover if the verbal was an expression of flesh and blood desires or a substitute for them.

"Shame on us," he said the first time he had shared her bed.

It was a moment for silence and a womanly smile.

"Are you Catholic?" he asked.

"No."

"It's still a sin."

"Do you really believe that?"

"With all my heart."

And he did. He was in an agony of remorse until he confessed to a priest that he had committed fornication. Deirdre was fascinated. He had cast her in multiple roles—his muse, his inspiration, now Jezebel. It was inevitable that they should soothe his conscience by talking of marriage. They became engaged and he made the announcement and only afterward did she tell him of Fritz.

"I'll get a divorce," she assured him.

"I don't believe in divorce."

"I never thought you were such a gung ho Catholic."

He stared at her. She had offended him. Good grief.

"Martin, I am kidding!"

"Kidding?"

"Of course, darling." She flew into his arms, laughing. "You thought I was serious, didn't you?"

For a frightening half minute she was hugging him but he was not hugging her. Then his arms closed around her. Deirdre swore to herself that she would never tell the truth again.

19 "MELISSA TOLD ME HOW TO get here." Kilmartin peeked around the door of Roger's office then stepped in. He looked around. "She's right. It has character."

"Meaning it's a mess. Sit down, sit down."

"It's hard to believe the stories she tells of you."

Roger was embarrassed. Martin Kilmartin was a poet whose work had earned him recognition on both sides of the Atlantic. That he should suggest that the distinction even of curiosity lay on Roger's side was ludicrous.

"Is it true you were a private investigator?"

"Oh, I still am. That is, I have a licence. My brother Phil is the senior partner."

"He still takes cases?"

"Only if they're interesting. No divorces."

Kilmartin sat back. "I should have thought that was the bulk of the business."

"It could be if you let it."

"I want to hire him. Or you. Whichever. There is something I must know."

As described, it was the sort of case Phil would normally reject out of hand. It spelled trouble. A man who was not sure a woman was joking when she said she was already married spelled trouble. If the woman was married, there was another man, and if the first man, like Martin, had been deceived, he would be unlikely to take it lightly. That Martin wished to take such measures to find out about Deirde Lacey made clear that he did not regard it lightly.

"And if she is married?"

"Do you realize I announced our engagement? If she is already married, that is an end to it, of course."

We live our lives on the border between the ridiculous and the sublime. That a writer who could wring the hearts of a reader because he had first wrung his own should be caught in such an absurd uncertainty was not right.

"Phil will find out. I'll have him come see you."

"At home."

"Of course. Or you could come to our place. We could go there now. Phil's home."

Roger's office was in Brownson Hall, also called Earth Sciences— "As opposed to heavenly?" Kilmartin asked—behind Sacred Heart and next to a parking lot from which he could easily reach his first-floor office. Brownson is as old as campus buildings get, but like everything else it had been remodeled and redone several times. Still, the office from which Roger could look out across the parking lot to St. Mary's lake had a nineteenth-century feel. He tried to reach Phil while Martin was with him, but Phil was not in the apartment.

"Do you think he will take the case?"

"I will urge him to."

Kilmartin wrung his hand in gratitude and they stepped gingerly out into a snowy world. It was an hour later that Roger talked with Phil.

"I can't take him as a client, Roger."

"Why not?"

"Oh, I'll find out what he wants. But I have already taken Deirdre Lacey for a client."

Deirdre had called the 800 number she found in the yellow pages of the Chicago directory and left a message. Phil had been fascinated that someone at Notre Dame should unwittingly contact him. He called Deirdre.

"Her hope, Roger, is that I will find that the man she married was married when he married her or has married since."

"Why?"

"A quiet divorce, removing the main impediment to her marrying Kilmartin."

Among the impenetrable mysteries of human existence are the reasons a man and woman are attracted to one another. Kilmartin could never have known anyone like Deirdre before coming to America, and Fritz, in the secondhand account Martin had given Roger, was as different from the poet as Hyperion from a Satyr.

"How does she expect you to locate this nomad?"

"Oh, he's here in South Bend. She seen him and is obviously frightened of him."

THE SEMESTER DREW TO A close, too soon for some, none too soon for others, the former largely students, the latter faculty by and large. Christmas parties were held. A wintry South Bend no longer exerted its magic and examinations loomed. The velleities of the previous months gave way to genuine resolution, and campus lights glowed as all-nighters were pulled, groups of students huddled together to make formulae and arguments and plots and characters adhere to the mind long enough to expel them into blue books. Hollow-eyed young women plodded across the campus walks to yet another examination, unshaven young men went red-eyed to their fate. And then, with the surprise of the last trump, the incredible happened. Examinations were over. The midsemester loomed. Sun-drenched beaches and far-flung places beckoned. Rejuvenated, the student body piled into their cars and drove away or took the shuttle to the airport and waited to be lifted homeward. In hours it seemed the campus was deserted. A light snow began to fall as if the silt of centuries were effacing all traces of the present and consigning to the past the year drawing to its close. Here and there a foreign student could be seen. But there loomed a more definitive shutdown when campus restaurants and the University Club and the Morris Inn would go on holiday.

It was in this midsemester limbo that Melissa Shaw became curious about the light under Martin Kilmartin's office on the seventh floor of Flanner Hall. Had he flown off to Dublin without turning it off? She told Branigan and they went up in the elevator together. But at the door, he hesitated.

"What's that smell?"

She had no idea. Wariness induced him to call the campus police and soon Katie Schwenk arrived on her bicycle exuding the insolence of office. She opened the door and almost immediately stepped back.

"Call the police!"

From the hallway, Melissa had seen Martin Kilmartin slumped over his desk. Katie hung up the phone that lay beside his hand, and prevented Branigan from going in. This was something for the South Bend Police.

"Is he dead?" Melissa managed to ask Katie Schwenk.

"Who are you?"

Melissa didn't answer the little campus cop. As for her own question, she knew the answer when she spoke. She left, hurrying down the hall, wanting the refuge of her own office.

PART TWO

1   LIEUTENANT STEWART, A SOUTH
Bend detective, was in charge of the investi-
gation, under orders from headquarters to wrap it up as quickly and
discreetly as possible. Chief Kocinski, who had risen through the
ranks from lowly patrolman as irresistibly as fumes rise from the
Ethanol plant west of town, held Notre Dame in awe. Among other
things, the university was the single greatest local employer and
members of the force either retired onto the campus police or picked
up bonuses directing traffic on football Saturdays. Don't bite the hand
that feeds you. While the medical examiner's crew went over the
scene, Stewart talked a bit with Melissa Shaw, although a bearded
professor kept interrupting. Mildly annoyed, Stewart took the elevator
to the basement where Branigan had his lair.

"You found the body?"

"I was there when it was found. A graduate student asked me to
check the office."

"Why?"

"She said the light was on. It was."

"Can you tell that in the daytime?"

"It was because she had noticed it at night that she became concerned."

That had struck Stewart as odd when he talked to the young
woman on the seventh floor. He would speak to her again when he
could get her away from her bearded protector. "Why were you concerned about a lighted window?" he had asked her, and the bearded
professor told her not to answer.

"Shouldn't there be a lawyer present?"

"Why?"

"To make sure Melissa's rights are respected."

A real nut. Did he think Melissa was suspected of a crime?

"Nice place you got here, Branigan," Stewart said when they reached the nether regions.

The building manager grinned. "I used to dream of retirement. Now I ask myself from what?" Concrete walls, clean and dry, pipes crisscrossing the ceiling, no window, but the neon lights made it seem daytime. Branigan seated himself at a desk but Stewart noticed the easy chair with magazines scattered around it. Nice.

"How long you worked here?"

Branigan consulted the inside of his eyelids. "Going on three years."

"What do you do exactly?"

Branigan told him, in detail. Stewart nodded. "Mainly faculty in the building?"

There was the university press, taking one floor of the eleven, and several institutes taking up others. The first floor housed student placement. But a lot of the floors were the offices of faculty, retired and still active. All those on seven were still active.

"Academically active," Branigan added, as if to be crystal clear.

"Tell me all about the seventh floor."

Flanner consisted of two joined towers so that each floor contained two connecting pods of offices. The body had been found in the western pod, where there were a dozen offices.

"Two corner ones. They're bigger."

"Who gets those?"

"Kilmartin was in one."

"You got keys to all the doors?"

"I only need one." Branigan plucked from his vest pocket the master key.

Stewart decided that Branigan really knew nothing of what went on in the building. Unless he used his master key to check out offices, but he wasn't going to admit that. Besides, who cared?

Upstairs again, Stewart talked with "Ice" Cubit the coroner and

112

Hupp of the ME team. A wide-eyed Katie Schwenk stood at attention beside Hupp.

"She says when she went into the office the phone was on the desk and she hung it up."

Stewart waited.

"My guess is that he was on the phone when he died."

"We know the cause of death, Ice?"

"Oh, it was heart."

Stewart looked at Hupp. "You want to know who he was on the phone with?"

"You'd think they would have reported it, wouldn't you?"

"Maybe he knocked the receiver off the cradle when he fell forward."

"A funny thing," Hupp said. He stepped closer to Stewart as if he didn't want to be overheard making a stupid remark. "The receiver? Someone must have sprayed it with pepper."

The body was taken away, all withdrew, and a funereal silence returned to the seventh floor of Flanner. Stewart was the last to leave. He checked out Kilmartin's phone and Hupp was right. It smelled heavily of pepper. A sneeze gathered and Stewart just got the phone into the cradle before it came, a head-clearing blast. Who was it that likened a sneeze to an orgasm? He didn't think he had read that in *Reader's Digest*, but you never know. He used his cell phone for the call he wanted to make.

2 WHEN THE PHONE RANG IN the apartment of the Knight brothers, which was located in graduate student housing, Roger was in the kitchen preparing a leg of lamb so Phil answered the phone.

"Enough there for three, Roger?" he called after a minute.

"Is it Greg?"

"No, Stewart. Jimmie Stewart."

Roger had to think a moment before he remembered the South Bend detective. He and Phil got along, enjoying a professional camaraderie.

"Invite him for dinner."

"I just did." Phil came into the kitchen. "I figured I could send out for something if there wasn't enough lamb."

"There's more than enough."

And so it was that Jimmie Stewart brought the news of the death of Martin Kilmartin to the Knight brothers. Phil had not known the poet so it was understandable that he discussed it with Stewart matter-of-factly. Roger sat in the middle of the couch, trying to absorb the news. Without bidding, the lines of Kilmartin's *Dies Irae* came to him.

"How long had he been dead?"

"Guessing, Cubit thinks two days, maybe more."

It was now Thursday. Roger thought back to the apparent time of death to find what he had been doing, as if that oriented the death of Martin Kilmartin. The poet had been so fragile, everyone had expected him to die young, yet the actual fact surprised, as death always does.

"May he rest in peace," Roger said.

And then he thought to call Father Carmody. There was lamb enough for four if the priest were free for dinner.

Father Carmody was fetched by Phil and Stewart while Roger tended the leg of lamb. When the priest came, his appetite seemed spurred by the news of a body discovered in a campus office. In pleasant silence, they settled to their dinner.

"This is the best lamb I have ever eaten, Roger," Father Carmody said.

Stewart also complimented the cook. When they rose from the table there was little left on the platter but a bone; the scalloped potatoes were gone, the broccoli consumed, and mint sauce melted on their plates. Phil was pouring cognac when the call from Cubit came. "His heart just exploded," he told the detective. "The condition he was in it wouldn't have taken much."

Stewart brought this lugubrious news to the others.

"A sneeze could have killed him," Roger said.

"Why do you say that?"

"Because it's true. He said so himself."

"There was a strong aroma of pepper on the receiver of his phone."

"Pepper?"

"A spray probably. I nearly sneezed out of my shoes myself when I was about to call out on it."

"Then he was murdered," Roger said deliberately. "Someone knew his condition and used pepper spray as a weapon."

"Who would do a thing like that?"

"I could make a list."

Phil said, "Before you do that I want to make a call."

The phone in Deirdre Lacey's apartment rang a dozen times before the recorded message came on. Phil replaced the phone.

"Jimmie, I think you and I should pay a visit."

When he and Roger were left alone, Father Carmody began to speak of deaths on campus, bodies not found for days, and gave his theory about the best time for someone at Notre Dame to die. The old priest hadn't really known Kilmartin, so, like Phil, he could speak of him almost casually, an instance of mortality, not the singular Irishman he had been.

"He was supposed to be in Ireland," Roger said. "He wanted to show Dublin to his fiancée."

"A young lady from here?"

"The one Phil has gone to check on."

The full significance of Phil's call to Deirdre now struck Roger. Phil was concerned for her because of what had happened to Kilmartin, and the two were linked, not merely as intended bride and groom, but because of the man Deirdre had hired Phil only a few days ago to check into, a man she had been married to.

"I am assuming it was not a valid marriage," the poet had said to Roger. He had come by Roger's office the previous week, showing up unannounced, still shaken by Deirdre's revelation that she had been married before. "Are American marriages valid? They went to some bureaucrat in the courthouse. A civil marriage. Do they count with the Church?"

"I'm not the one to ask. But if it does?"

"I can't marry her, of course."

This possibility did not seem to devastate the poet as much as it might have. Phil was not a Catholic and shared with Deirdre the feeling that a mountain was being made of a molehill. He had heard her side of the story on Monday.

"Now she wishes she hadn't told him. What if she hadn't, Roger, and they went ahead and got married and he finds out later? What then?"

"What do you mean?"

"Are they married or not?"

"Phil, I think you have a vocation. Become a Catholic and devote yourself to the study of canon law."

Phil was made uncomfortable by any suggestion that he make so drastic a decision as conversion. Roger was sure that some day his brother would come into the Church, but it would be a day when it was less foreign to him than it still was.

"Well, it doesn't matter, Roger. She told him about the husband, mainly because he had shown up in South Bend and she didn't feel safe with him running around loose. He sounds like a Hell's Angels type."

"What exactly are you to do?"

"Find out why he is here."

"And then?"

"That depends on why he is here."

"Why does she think he's here?"

Phil tipped his head to the side. "To rough her up. Maybe more. She is definitely frightened. She left him because of that sort of thing."

The story conjured up the image of young men and women drifting about the country, forming temporary alliances, breaking up and going off in different directions and contracting other temporary alliances and so on to infinity. Only that is not what life is, an ever open vista in which our past plays no role in the present and future. Quite apart from a religious perspective, the nomadic life Deirdre had led with her husband Fritz was unworthy of a human being. We are meant to introduce direction and sense into our lives. Even pagans know this. It said much for Deirdre that she had escaped, had educated herself, and was continuing to distance herself from the heedless days with Fritz.

3 ⟶ SHAMROCK RESIDENCES WAS
one of a dozen developments in an area east of
the university once called Dogpatch that provided housing for students who chose not to live on campus. These developments had
replaced ramshackle single dwellings and their proximity to campus
put them within walking distance for the hardy. Deirdre Lacey had
considered and then rejected the possibility of sharing an apartment
with three other graduate women in the housing provided by the
university. It was one thing to become a student again as she approached thirty, it was something else to become completely assim-
ilated to students almost a decade younger than herself. Besides,
Deirdre had gained self-confidence as the result of her studies at
Madison and her association with Notre Dame. The autonomy of
having her own apartment appealed to her.

"Two bedrooms!" Martin had cried, when he came to inspect it.
"You should sublet."

"If I wanted company I would be in graduate student housing."

"I will take that as a rebuff."

That was in September. Deirdre was used to being flirted with. For
reasons she never understood, men felt compelled to act amorously
around her, and Kilmartin had then seemed merely one more insin-
cere swain. It had never occurred to her that he would become serious. When he began to speak of marriage, it might have been an
extended joke, but then out of the blue he announced their engagement to the assembled faculty and students of Celtic Studies, and
that he was taking her to Dublin as a pre-wedding trip.

She might have kept silent about Fritz, dismissing it as something past, dead and buried, but then, like a monster in a bad dream, Fritz himself had suddenly confronted her. She had just parked and gotten out of her car, not paying any attention to the pickup parked a few places away. But when he hopped out of it, as agile as a boy, and came toward her, she froze in her tracks. Her first mad impulse was that he must not learn where she lived.

As they drove, Phil Knight recounted to Jimmie Stewart the young woman's description of the returned husband. It had been told vividly—the ponytail, the open leather jacket, tattoos peeking through the chest hair visible because of the open black shirt, boots.

"What did he say?"

"Long time no see."

But his very presence was a threat. Martin Kilmartin had announced that they would marry and here was an insuperable obstacle to that, presuming Fritz hadn't divorced her, but why would he have bothered if she herself had not? How do you divorce someone when you don't even know where they are? And if they're gone, what's the point of divorce? That is how she had rationalized it until Fritz materialized like the bad luck she had never been able to evade for long.

"Did you tell Kilmartin?" Phil had asked her.

"Yes," she replied.

"And?"

"He doesn't think it matters. I mean, he hopes it isn't an impediment because of the way I was married. He is a very devout Catholic."

"Maybe he's right." Phil had picked up at secondhand much Catholic lore ever since Roger had been converted to Catholicism when he was a graduate student at Princeton.

Phil's reaction when he met Deirdre for the first time was to make clear it was the last. No sooner was she seated at their table in the

120

University Club then she said with a nervous laugh, "I want you to investigate my husband?"

"Miss Lacey," Phil began, intending to be equally abrupt in return.

"I mean I want you to find out if a man is my husband."

That caught his interest of course and over lunch he listened to the saga of the little girl from Minnesota who had run off with a motorcyclist, married him, and then deserted him.

"How long ago was that?"

"Seven years. Almost eight."

"And you haven't seen him since?"

"Once. In Madison. Twice, counting the other day."

"Had he been looking for you?"

She thought he had, that he had tracked her down. Since her phone and apartment were in her maiden name, it would have been easy enough for him to do that, once he got to South Bend.

"What else would have brought him to South Bend?"

"He's a hockey fan."

If there was a sport for which Phil's enthusiasm was under control it was hockey. Still, the Notre Dame team played a good schedule and a home stand usually delivered first-rate entertainment.

"Notre Dame hockey?"

"That's his story. But he thought Lefty Smith was still coach."

"What exactly did he want?"

"I don't know. That's why I'm worried."

"Any idea where he's staying."

"Some motel over the Michigan border."

Despite the oddity of the case, it was not the sort of thing Phil stirred himself into activity for. Nor did there seem to be any prospect of remuneration sufficient to offset his misgivings.

"How much do you charge?" she asked, as if reading his throughts.

"Look, I don't think I'm the one to do this."

"If it's a matter of money, I can afford it."

How much did she think it would cost? Phil was telling her it was not a matter of money, when she interrupted. "I can give you ten thousand dollars now and more later."

"And wipe out your savings?"

"I haven't told you everything."

When she deserted Fritz years ago, she had in her haste grabbed his backpack instead of her own, a mistake she hadn't realized until she was in the rest room of the bus bearing her away. She opened the backpack—they had bought identical ones—and stared at a sack full of money.

"Fifty-dollar bills. Hundred-dollar bills. All so new they didn't even look real."

"Where would he have gotten it?"

"I don't know. I closed the bag right away and sat there trying to think of ways to get it back to him that wouldn't tell him which way I was heading. In the end, I just kept it."

"How much money was it?"

She was silent for a moment, her eyes very round. "Over three hundred thousand dollars. I counted it."

"I'm surprised it took him so long to find you."

"Will you help me?"

"Where is the money now?"

"In the trunk of my car."

"Is there somewhere you can stay, somewhere other than your apartment?"

She didn't like the idea, but she saw the wisdom of staying away from her apartment. "He already broke in once to search it, trying not to make a mess, as if I wouldn't notice."

She arranged to stay with Melissa Shaw.

"Will you take care of the money for me?"

She apparently had no idea what she was asking him to do. Even to suggest another hiding place was to become her accomplice. By her own admission she had stolen the money from Fritz. Well, she kept it after realizing what she had done. Good Lord, imagine driving around with that kind of money in her car. Suddenly the very implausibility of the car trunk seemed an assurance of safety. He suggested she just leave it where it was for now.

They had arrived at Deirdre's apartment. Jimmie Stewart had listened to Phil's account without comment. Now he said, "So why are we coming here?"

"She only stayed with Melissa one night. She obviously didn't go to Dublin with Kilmartin."

The door of the apartment was slightly ajar and Phil pushed it fully open. Jimmie let Phil go first. Neither felt any impulse to announce their arrival.

The living room was a mess, the cushions of the couch and chairs slashed open, a coffee table upended. The kitchen was worse, the floor littered with broken china and pots and pans, the cabinet doors standing open, their shelves denuded. The room Deirdre used for a study was a clutter of books that had been swept from the shelves. The monitor of her computer stared blankly at them. But the bedroom was the worst. Rugs, bedding, clothes were everywhere and the mattress cut open.

"I don't think he got the money," Jimmie said.

Phil took out his notebook, found a page, and read off some numbers. "That's her licence tag. Would you put out a search for it."

"Wasn't it outside?"

Phil shook his head.

4   THE DIXIE MOTEL WAS SO
named because the highway on which it stood
had originally been the historic north/south Dixie Highway. To say
the establishment had fallen on evil days might suggest that it had
once known a golden period. It had been seedy from the beginning,
a jerry-built structure thrown up in the hope of attracting Notre Dame
football fans whose elation or despondency after games would blind
them to the modesty of their rooms. But this hope had been undercut
by the sudden and simultaneous construction of more elegant estab-
lishments nearer to campus. Before the building of those new motels
and hotels and condominiums, the Dixie could have counted on being
packed on football weekends and that would have offset the doldrums
that characterized the rest of the year. Its original hopes dashed, the
motel had been saved by offering weekly and monthly rates and thus
had become home to a clientele whose mobility was episodic and for
whom a month or two in the Dixie at its affordable rates had its
charms. Pickups were parked by the unit doors. The office was located in a self-standing structure that had the look of a guardhouse.
It was in the office, wary behind his messy desk, that Gilbert Plaisance had received Phil Knight on the day after Deirdre had hired
him to find Fritz Davis.

"A private detective," he said, after studying the licence Phil had
shown him.

"I just want to ask you a few questions."

"I don't have to answer them."

Phil ignored that. "Get many cyclists here?"

"Cyclists!"

"People on motorcycles."

The question had stirred Plaisance from his wariness. "You after them?"

"Tell me about it."

Plaisance stood and said he would show him. They crossed the parking lot which had been covered with a thin coat rather than retarred and now the cracks and crevices were emerging from disguise. The unit to which Plaisance took him was a sty. The television lay smashed in a corner, broken furniture littered the floor, awful prints hung awry on the walls and there seemed to have been a flood in the bathroom.

"A fight, one helluva fight. But I only heard of it the following day after they're gone. People were in the next unit but they were too scared to let me know what was going on."

"Cyclists?"

"Yes." They walked back to the office. "Weird, weird guys. We get some odd ones here, this isn't exactly the Marriott, but this bunch were like that Marlon Brando movie, know what I mean?"

"How did they register?"

This was embarrassing for Plaisance. He tried various ways of explaining it but every time it came out that he sometimes bilked the owner out of the rent money by not registering everyone who was staying. "I mean, if it's a week or more, of course, they're going to sign the book. But there are people who wouldn't give their right name even if they did register."

So Plaisance had supplemented his income by pocketing the rent of some guests. The motorcyclists—there had only been two plus a girl, although Plaisance made it sound like the invasion of Rommel's desert corps—had paid cash, not getting off their bikes when they stopped by Plaisance's window. He gave them keys, took their money, put it in his shoe, and had a beer to celebrate the bonus.

"How you going to explain the wrecked unit?"

"My story is they threatened me when I demanded they pay first so I let them in."

His description of the cyclist who had paid for the room sounded like Fritz Davis. "How about the other guy?"

"My theory is they fought over the girl."

The trio had settled into the unit and Plaisance had settled down with the twelve-pack of warm beer he kept under his desk. He had preferred warm beer from the time he worked in the pasteurizing room of a brewery.

"You didn't hear the fight?"

"Even cold sober I wouldn't have. That unit could be in the next county it's so far from the office. I usually stash my guests as far back as possible." His guests were those whose rent ended up in his shoe.

After he drove out of the Dixie Motel, Phil called Melissa Shaw in her office on his cell phone. The fact that he was Roger's brother was enough to make her receptive.

"Is Deirdre staying with you?"

"She spent last night in the apartment. At your suggestion, she said."

"Did she say she was leaving?"

Melissa seemed to ponder the significance of the question. "No. She was still in bed when I left."

"And did she tell you her problem?"

"An old flame threatening her."

"What's the number of your apartment?"

But no one answered when he called there. Deirdre might not want to answer the phone for a number of reasons. He decided to check it out. Most of the things he did on a job were pointless.

Fifteen minutes later, Phil pulled up to a building identical to that in which he and Roger lived but at the far end of graduate student housing. The car Deirdre had driven out of the University Club parking lot after their lunch was parked in front of the unit.

The sight of it chased away the apprehension with which he had driven from the Dixie Motel. Fritz had hit the road and Deirdre was safe and sound in Melissa's apartment. Soon she and Kilmartin would be off for Dublin. He put the car in gear and went home. It was a decision he would come to blame himself for later, after Kilmartin's body was found and Deirdre was missing.

Roger dismissed Phil's sense of delinquency. "Phil. If you had rung the door bell no one would have answered and you would have drawn the same conclusion you did when the phone wasn't answered."

"I could have asked Melissa to check out the apartment."

This self-recrimination returned when Phil took Jimmie to where Deirdre's car had been parked. No need to start a search for it if it wasn't gone. It was parked where he had last seen it, in front of the unit where Melissa lived, although Deirdre had spent only one night there. Jimmie called the police garage but before the vehicle was taken away he had the trunk opened. He and Phil stood side by side when they looked into the trunk. It was empty.

"You ever see the money?" Jimmie asked.

"No."

"She pay you the ten thousand?"

"No."

"You say the biker's name was Fritz Davis. We better find him."

Jimmie's suggestion implied that when they found Fritz they would find Deirdre. What wasn't clear was what any of this had to do with the death of Martin Kilmartin.

5

BRANIGAN GOT MOST OF IT
from Mrs. Bumstead, the secretary in Celtic
Studies. Prudie was indignant because of the way they talked about
the man they were looking for.

"They're supposed to be so high-minded and fair, but they're worse
than anybody. They've got it all figured out that the man Deirdre
Lacey was married to did it, and why? Because he wears leather, has
a ponytail, and rides a motorcycle."

Branigan clucked in sympathy and shook his head. Of course Prudie was thinking of that weird son of hers with the rainbow-colored
hair and vacant expression.

"I guess she just ditched him years ago, but of course he's the
one they talk about. She's making eyes at every man in sight and
one of them says they're getting married and all along she's got a
husband."

"The biker."

"She deserts him and he's the villain." Prudence Bumstead was
the kind of woman who despised other women whenever she had a
choice.

"They give his name?"

"Fitz something. Wouldn't that make him Irish?"

Branigan said nothing but he had no doubt that the man they were
looking for was the giant he had run into in Fiametti's, just across
the state line where Branigan went on Sundays when he wanted to
drink without having to order a meal to do it. Sunday or not, Branigan
got into his work clothes when he went to Fiametti's. The patrons
were from the trailer parks along the highway or the el cheapo motels

that catered to itinerant workers. He became aware of a man at the bar staring at him. The man's belly emerged from the unzipped leather jacket like an airbag that had gone off accidentally. Except that Fritz drove a bike not a car. He came over to Branigan's table as if to give him a better look at his belly.

"You work at Notre Dame?"

Behind the bar, Millie looked away. Had she been trying to impress this giant with the suggestion that she had some high-toned customers?

"I'm caretaker of one of the buildings."

The big man pulled out a chair, twirled it around with one hand and then straddled it, moving close to the edge of the table. A great hand came out and Branigan took it.

"Fritz. Fritz Davis."

Branigan told him his name. He still wasn't sure whether or not this was someone who had a grudge against the Irish and wanted to take it out on him. But the big guy seemed genuinely interested in what it was like to work on a university campus. Branigan was a little subdued at first, thinking Fritz might want to apply for a job and he couldn't encourage that. On the other hand, he didn't want to tell this guy that there was no way he could get a job at Notre Dame. But that wasn't it either. Branigan ordered a pitcher of beer, Frtiz turned his chair around, lit what didn't smell like a cigarette, and they settled in. Almost immediately Millie came running over.

"You can't smoke that in here," she hissed, directing the words at Branigan.

"Sorry about that." Fritz pinched the roach and dropped it into her shirt pocket. Millie danced back, fanning her shirt, but she was laughing. She made a beeline for the back room to get rid of it.

"Flanner," he said, when Fritz asked him the name of his building. Branigan hadn't gotten this much attention in years. At home they were sick of the stories he brought from campus and not even his wife shared his sense of holding down an important job. Fritz didn't blink when Branigan told him he was in complete charge of an eleven-story building where he had an office in the basement and a staff of four. The cleaning ladies might not have liked being called his staff, but it was difficult not to rise to the level of Fritz's admiring curiosity.

"I'm the one who should envy you," Branigan said magnanimously. "Hop on a bike and just hit the road." He shook his head.

"You ride a bike?"

"I wouldn't even dare try."

"Dare? Hell, women ride them."

His head half-turned to the girl at the bar whose straight blonde hair hung to her tailbone. "People live there, students, is that it?"

"It used to be a residence hall," Branigan conceded, "but it's been turned into offices."

"Teachers?"

"Professors."

"And you're in charge?"

That's when Branigan got out the master key and told Fritz that this little baby could get him through any door in the building. The point was that he was trusted. No one worried that he might go into an office and, well, look around or take something.

"It's a completely professional arrangement." He let Fritz look at the key which he had separated from the others on the ring. Millie arrived with the pitcher Fritz had ordered, squeezing between them with a girlish laugh. Fritz slapped her rear end when she headed back to the bar and she laughed some more. Fritz handed Branigan his keys.

On Monday Branigan got out his keys and had difficulty when he tried to open the door of Prudence Bumstead's office.

"What's wrong?" Her tone had changed from the shamefaced one in which she had told him she had forgotten her key. Branigan had gone up on the elevator with her only to find that there was no master key on his ring. Melissa Shaw came along in a couple of minutes and she opened the door and Branigan got out of there. He spent an hour in the main building getting a replacement from campus security.

"You lose the other one?"

"It's probably in a pocket I haven't searched yet."

"Well, bring this back when you find your own."

It wasn't until Martin Kilmartin's death a couple days later turned up the fact that Deirdre Lacey was also missing and that the police were looking for her first husband, a bearded giant named Fritz Davis, that Branigan put two and two together. Fritz had had time to remove the master key from the ring while Millie was giggling over the pitcher of beer.

He knew he should tell the police but he didn't. He drove out to Fiametti's on a weeknight and asked Millie if the bearded biker had been back but she couldn't remember him.

"He slapped your bottom."

"Big deal."

She made it sound as if giving her a pat was a bonus for ordering a pitcher.

6

PADRAIG MALONEY CRIED helplessly when Stewart talked to him about Martin Kilmartin's death.

"I thought the man was in Ireland."

"So he must have had reservations. What airline?"

Maloney tucked in his chin, his cheekbones wet with the tears that had continued down into his beard. "Aer Lingus, I'm sure."

But the airline had no reservation to Dublin for Martin Kilmartin and Deirdre Lacey, together or separately. Maloney sobbed again and Melissa wished he would take it easy. He looked guilty as sin.

"It's all my fault," he said to Stewart.

"How so?"

"I'm the one who admitted that woman to special status so she could follow courses."

"What woman is that?"

"The one he said he was going to marry. Deirdre Lacey. Oh, she had a transcript from Wisconsin and she wasn't applying for student status, but what did we really know about her?"

Melissa was shocked, not just because he was as much as accusing Deirdre of harming Martin but because he himself had been mooning over Deirdre for months, following the progress of Kilmartin's conquest of her, muttering as he watched them slip into the poet's car for a smoke. Reflections on the windshield made it impossible to know what they were up to, but the cigarette smoke coming from the cracked windows made that obvious. For him to point the finger at Deirdre now did more than make Melissa uneasy. She could not resist thinking that Maloney was making himself look responsible.

"The door of his office was locked?" Lieutenant Stewart asked.

"They lock when they're shut."

"So how could anyone get inside?"

"With a key?"

"But who would have had a key?"

"Who opened the door when you found the body, Melissa?"

"Branigan."

The detective just listened, not reacting at all, one way or the other. Melissa waited for Professor Maloney to tell the detective that there were copies of all the keys of those in Celtic Studies right here in the office of the director. But he didn't. Melissa left; she went down in the elevator and out into the chill December air. Then she sat on a bench and watched her breath escape like tobacco smoke from her lips when she breathed.

While they waited for the police to come, after she had fetched Branigan and he in turn had fetched Katie Schwenk, the campus cop had told Melissa of the smell of the telephone. Was that what Branigan had smelled when they first approached the door? With her first serious cold of the season, Melissa could not even smell the fumes from the ethanol plant anymore.

"Did you know him?" Katie had whispered when they had gone down the hall, away from Branigan.

"Yes."

"What a case of halitosis he had."

"I never noticed."

"His telephone reeked. Smelled like pepper."

"Pepper!"

"I mean a bad smell."

"But like pepper?"

"That was my impression. Did you smell anything funny?"

For answer, Melissa sniffled. Katie handed her a tissue.

Melissa had noticed Katie hanging up the phone before she closed

Martin Kilmartin's office door and said they would wait for the para-medics and the South Bend police to come.

Melissa had slipped away to Celtic Studies, telling Katie where she would be. The door of the inner office was closed and a light on the phone suggested that Maloney was in there. Melissa sat at Mrs. Bumstead's desk and tried not to think. But the mention of pepper recalled those occasions when Kilmartin and others had said that something as innocent as a sneeze could carry him off. Hadn't Arne joked about turning in some poems over which he had sprinkled some pepper? But mainly it had been Martin himself who spoke of his fragile hold on life, his enlarged heart, the menace of the simplest things. How could this not endear him to her more, and, she sup-posed, to Deirdre as well. Deirdre had looked almost as surprised as anyone else when Martin announced that he intended to marry her. It was like becoming engaged to someone on their deathbed, and all the more romantic for that. Martin's tenuous hold on life should have affected Padraig Maloney's attitude toward their rivalry for Deirdre: he could lose in the short term and win in the long. And where was she herself in all this?

Women students did not often admit it but there was always an element of flirtation involved when the professor was male. Sometimes on his side only and thus unwelcome, sometimes on hers and thus unserious but fun nonetheless. She was half in love with Roger Knight and Padraig Maloney as she had been with Martin Kilmartin. Why couldn't she respond to the attentions of Arne Jensen or Brian Elliot?

Arne had actually tried to write a poem for her whereas Brian had wanted to take her places, to dinner, to games, and finally to his parents home in Midlothian, Michigan, for Thanksgiving. Her parents in Delaware had been reconciled to her decision not to come home when she told them she had been invited to Midlothian.

"Another student?"

"Yes."

No need to say a male and an undergraduate at that. By all rights,

Arne and Brian should regard her as half a faculty member herself, but she wasn't a year older than either of them, enough to savor the pleasures of the big sister when she wasn't leading them on. In Midlothian, she got along with everybody, but Brian's father was particularly kind.

"Brian tells me you steered him toward Roger Knight."

Had she? "He's a wonderful professor."

"I know him a bit. I know his brother Phil better. I want Roger to be the director of a center I am being asked to finance at Notre Dame, in honor of Malachy O'Neill. Have you ever heard of him?"

"From Roger Knight."

"O'Neill had the greatest impact on me of any prof at Notre Dame."

An almost identical statement was made by Donald Weber, a professor at the local college and a domer besides who was another Thanksgiving dinner guest. He and Elliot seemed to compete with one another to say the most outrageously favorable things about Malachy O'Neill.

"I was in the classroom when he died," Weber said, and it seemed a trump he had played before. Elliot fell silent and then left the room. For fifteen minutes she fended off Weber's effort to get her to admit that Notre Dame was not a fraction of what it had once been.

When she and Brian were getting ready to return to South Bend, James Elliot asked Melissa to put pressure on Roger Knight to accept the directorship of the Malachy O'Neill Center.

"I doubt that he would make such a decision on the basis of anything I said."

"Don't sell yourself short. We never know the influence we have with others."

When she brought up the visit to Midlothian and out of a sense of duty turned the topic to Malachy O'Neill, Roger seized the opportunity to talk about the house in the Chicago suburb and the cache of papers.

"If nothing else, they have great historical value. Greg Whelan, the archivist, is in seventh heaven."

"I suppose they'll end up in the new center?"

"I don't know."

"You could insist on it."

The Ballad of Pearl Harbor had been making the rounds on the seventh floor of Flanner, recited derisively by those encouraged by Kilmartin's alleged negative assessment of the poem. Melissa had read a stanza or two but it just wasn't her sort of thing. She didn't mean it was bad, or good, she just didn't like ballads. Roger nodded as she told him this.

"That is his longest poem, and probably one of the earliest. But he was a foe of free verse, there's no doubt of that. He was attracted by the most demanding forms and with practice sometimes worked within the restraints to good effect. But I doubt that anyone would call him a major poet."

A minor poet? Roger took that to be a significant category. Minor poets were to be distinguished from the occasional writer of verse.

"Of course almost all writers produce poetry. Is Cardinal Newman a poet? Is Melville or Updike? Failure to count as a major poet doesn't make one a bad poet."

When asked to name other writers not known for their poetry who had nonetheless written it, Roger grinned. "Max Brand."

"The western writer?"

"And the author of *Dr. Kildare.* Yes, he longed to be a poet and produced yards of quasi-classical poetry."

They were getting away from Malachy O'Neill. "Brian's father asked me to pressure you to accept the directorship of the proposed O'Neill Center."

"He may be the only man alive who can imagine me in an administrative position."

"You could do it."

"Right now I am more concerned with what has happened to Deirdre Lacey."

Immediately Melissa felt terrible. Had it really sunk in that Deirdre was missing, perhaps worse . . .

7

THE PUBLICATION OF SEVERAL of Malachy O'Neill's poems in *The Observer* called forth pages of harsh and hilarious comments. A contest was initiated inviting imitation O'Neill verse. Becky Fontana was sure that Sauer was behind it all, particularly when her colleague produced a tongue-in-cheek essay comparing the poetry of Malachy O'Neill with that "yardstick of campus poetry," the verse of the Rev. Charles L. O'Donnell, C.S.C. He ended with the suggestion that readers who wished to rinse their aesthetic palate after tasting these two might turn with profit to the poetry of the late, lamented Martin Kilmartin.

"Of course he despised Kilmartin when he was alive, advising students not to waste time on his courses. 'Quite amateur,' was his verdict. Now he has become his champion."

"Another dead white male?"

But Becky would not rise to Roger's gentle joshing. She was not a feminist, merely an extremely gifted young woman. Nor did she have any quarrel with the Western Canon, particularly when she saw the candidates to replace it.

"That's the danger, Roger. Look at this silly letter by Donald Weber, extolling O'Neill's poetry to the skies."

"I hadn't seen that."

"He compares it favorably with that of Kilmartin. Of course he is answering Sauer without mentioning him."

"Weber seems a bit of a chameleon. Wasn't he here a few weeks ago feeding Sauer with negative anecdotes about Malachy O'Neill?"

There was method in Weber's madness, as became clear when

David Simmons stopped by. The university fund-raiser was distraught because the death of Martin Kilmartin was no longer being treated as a natural one.

"That's all we need, a murder investigation on campus." Doubtless Simmons was thinking of the effect of such an investigation on his efforts to attract donations to the university. "Mendax is raising hell with the police I can tell you."

Mendax was the university counsel, a lawyer who seemed to model herself on the more preposterous legal dramas on television. But she was a formidable foe nonetheless, as many had discovered to their sorrow. Whether her zeal would have been less were she representing those suing the university was an open question, but her zeal once purchased was certain.

"Of course she is concentrating on the newspaper accounts."

"David, I myself think he was murdered."

"What!"

"Someone had sprayed his telephone with pepper."

Incredulity assumed different forms on David's face. "Pepper! This amounts to murder?"

"In this case, deliberately done, knowing the condition of Kilmartin's health, yes."

"Have you suggested this to anyone?"

"David, it was generally known that it would have taken little more than a sneeze to bring on a fatal heart attack."

"But do the police know?"

"Yes."

"Oh my God!"

Simmons lived in the world of appearance, of what people think, of reputation, ranking, and public perception. How as a matter of fact Kilmartin had died signified less than what people thought had happened. The idea of a murder having been committed on the campus was inconceivable to one whose task it was to present the university in roseate unreal colors. Institutions themselves now occupied this wonderland where nothing is but what is thought. *Esse non est percipi,* Roger might have said to someone other than the flustered member of the Notre Dame Foundation.

"Has James Elliot spoken to you about these matters?"

"He has been more concerned about the attacks on Malachy O'Neill."

"Sauer! Is there nothing sacred for that man?"

"William Butler Yeats, apparently."

Sauer, having savaged the favorite professor of many alumni, had disarmingly proposed that the university celebrate the anniversary of the appearance of Yeats on the Notre Dame campus. Sauer apparently knew nothing of the first visit and was thinking of that which took place under the presidency of Charles O'Donnell. Pending approval, Greg Whelan had begun to assemble materials from the archives for a display should the commemoration take place.

"I thought I would include some verse by Yeats's host."

"Father O'Donnell."

"Yes."

"Wonderful."

"I have also found a tribute to Yeats by Malachy O'Neill that would be appropriate."

Greg said these things, which surely would have sounded subversive to Professor Sauer, in his most matter-of-fact tone.

"There's one by Auden you might use as well."

Roger had come to the archives to see how the inventory of the O'Neill papers was going and Greg now turned to the work he had been doing on them.

"He was a keeper. He must have kept every student paper turned in to him. His requirement was that the student prepare two copies, one for marking, the other for keeping. Sometimes O'Neill kept both copies. Take a look at this."

Greg had taken a sheaf of typewritten sheets from a large envelope and began to shuffle through them.

"Are those student essays?"

Greg nodded. And then he had found what he was looking for, an essay by James Elliot. He handed it to Roger. It was seven pages double-spaced, a study of Gerard Manley Hopkins' *Windhover*. The complete poem stood at the beginning of the essay and it was quoted copiously throughout. "The poem is the best comment on the poem," Elliot wrote, putting the maxim in quotation marks.

"One of O'Neill's repeated bits of wisdom."

"There's some truth in it."

"It made writing essays easier."

The copy Greg had handed him was unmarked so it was impossible to know what judgment Malachy O'Neill had made of it. There was no essay by Donald Weber in the same batch, which surprised Roger. They had been classmates and both had taken O'Neill's class.

"Are there papers for O'Neill's last class?"

Greg nodded and reached for another envelope. Roger easily found the proposal for an essay that Donald Weber, returned from the wars, now a graduate student, had submitted to O'Neill. It had been commented on with a red pencil. Weber had proposed to write on Pound. "Nonsense!!!" was printed in block letters across the front page. On the backs of the typewritten pages O'Neill had written a passionate plea against pedantry, telling Weber that he ran the risk of picking up the worst traits of the graduate student and academic critic, erecting a great screen of supposed erudition between the reader and the poem. He ended with the promise to give Weber an A if he would agree not to write the proposed essay. A complete putdown stated with unfeigned passion. Roger passed it to Greg.

"Didn't he say Malachy O'Neill was his favorite professor?"

"Maybe he profited from this advice."

But the following day, Greg called to say he had an interesting addendum to what they had been speaking of.

"I found a note from Weber to O'Neill."

"I'll come over."

"Don't be silly. I need some fresh air. I'll make a photocopy and bring it to you."

And so Greg came to Roger's office in the Earth Sciences building just behind Sacred Heart Church and the Main Building. He drove, pulling into a place just outside Roger's window. Greg handed the photocopy to Roger and then prowled his bookshelves while he read it.

Dear Professor O'Neill,

I still cannot believe the unjust and arrogant comments you made on my proposed essay. Perhaps you were not quite yourself when you wrote them. Maybe you have forgotten writing them. I return them to you now so that you can get some idea what a devastating effect they had on someone who came to your class after some years away from Notre Dame carrying wonderful memories of your teaching when I was an undergraduate. In the meantime you have become remote and bitter. I understand now, as I could not before, the awful reputation you have acquired among your colleagues as well as among many, many students. Quite apart from the manner of your reaction, I think what you say in these comments is absurd. I cannot believe you wrote them. I appeal from O'Neill drunk to O'Neill sober. I will await your reply.

Disappointedly,
Donald Weber

P.S. When I was in Navy boot camp we had a chief who displayed the same phony omniscience that characterizes your comments. Several of us took him aside one night and administered the appropriate punishment. Perhaps something similar is coming to you at last.

"Well, well," Roger said when he had read the letter.
"Notice the date."
Donald Weber had sent his disappointed, and threatening, letter to Malachy O'Neill the day before the legendary professor's final class, a class it had long been Weber's boast that he had attended.

8

PADRAIG MALONEY HAD BEEN refused access to Martin Kilmartin's office by Lieutenant Stewart, who was unimpressed by Maloney's reminder that he was the acting director of the program in which Kilmartin had been a visitor, and his claim to be as close as kin to the dead poet.

"There's nothing in there anyway. It's as empty an office as I have ever seen. A desk, a file cabinet, a few books." Stewart worked his lips. "No telephone. That's been taken as evidence."

"Evidence of what?"

"I'm just a cop, professor. You'll have to ask the prosecutor."

"Lieutenant, you can be with me when I go in. I want to get the student papers for last semester."

"Hadn't he turned in his grades?"

Martin Kilmartin had turned in his grades, a copy of which came to Maloney as acting director. The poet had been a severe grader, doubtless not yet acclimated to the grade inflation that was now epidemic coast to coast. His highest grade had been an A−, there had been two B's, and the rest, save for one D, C's. Once that would have been an unsurprising spread. Nowadays few students received less than a B, at least half received A's. A semblance of discrimination was retained by using + and −, giving effectively six grades without any need to employ C or D. Melissa had received a B from Kilmartin, Arne Jensen the D. He had come to Maloney asking to get back the work he had submitted to Kilmartin, hence Maloney's request for access to the office.

"You mean he's got some poems you turned in?"

Arne blushed marvelously, his rounded cheeks looking white

against the upsurge of self-conscious blood. "He was going to make some comments."

"I see you got a D." Maloney had found the carbon of Kilmartin's grades.

"Did anyone get an A?"

Maloney shook his head. "One A minus."

"I'll bet that was Melissa."

"You don't expect me to answer that question, do you?"

"I know she did."

"Well, you're wrong. She got a B." Maloney formed the plosive silently before saying it aloud.

"The sonofabitch."

"*De mortuis non nisi bonum.*"

"I'm not Catholic," Arne said, annoyed.

Maloney roared. "Do you think everything in Latin is Catholic? How about *e pluribus unum*? How about *Habeas corpus*?"

"I submitted one of her poems. He gave Melissa a D."

Meaning that this no longer blushing, seething Scandinavian had been awarded a B by the late Kilmartin. What did it prove? He told Arne he would check and see if it was okay with the police to take things from the office of the dead man and, after being refused by Stewart, he decided to use the copy of Kilmartin's key that was kept in the director's office.

"Come on," he said to Arne Jensen, heading down the hall to the corner office that still had yellow tape across it. Maloney unpeeled one end of two banners and put the key in the lock. "You realize we're breaking the law?"

"What law?"

"Good question." He turned the key and pushed inside. Over his shoulder he said, "No need to turn on the light. Shut the door behind you."

Martin seemed more present in his absence than he had the day his body had been found here. Wintry light illumined the room, the late December sun was low in the sky but its rays found the earth too distant to warm or brighten. In shadow the office did not look so functional. The horseshoe metal desk, the gimmicky chair, the sideways file cabinets—Kilmartin had done nothing to put his imprint on this space, except for a few books scattered on the shelves attached to the wall. Maloney noticed that one of the books was a paperback of one of Kilmartin's collections. Parents left children when they died but poets left verse, a questionable immortality in either case. One could walk among the stacks on the eighth floor of the library, through centuries of British and American literature, the vast majority of the books untouched and unread as they aged. In some sense their authors lived on, but is an unread book a book in the full sense of the term? For a while at least, Martin would continue to be read. Maloney took the paperback and it opened at *Dies Irae*.

"I don't see any papers." Arne had slid open the file cabinet drawers, one after another, as if he were checking bodies at the morgue.

Maloney sat in Martin's chair with a sense of usurpation, almost sacrilege, and opened a deep drawer full of papers. "Voilà." He had to stop Arne, who reached into the drawer. "I'll do that. We have to respect the privacy of the other students."

Maloney went through the stack of papers like a teller counting bills. "Here you are." As he handed the paper to Arne, he saw the neatly lasered lines of a sonnet.

"That is Melissa's," Arne said. "Find the one with her name on it."

"Go around to the other side of the desk."

Melissa's paper was on the bottom of the stack. There were four lines under a capitalized LOVE SONG. Maloney looked at Arne, who was leaning across the desk. Again a blush suffused the nordic face.

"I'll read it." He cleared his throat and read.

> *Your honeyed appellation is sweet upon my ear,*
> *It sounds my depths and penetrates to where*
> *The sweetest treasure waits, stolen*
> *From your flower's dusty pollen.*

"He gave it a B."

"That's my poem."

Maloney chuckled. "No wonder you got a D."

"But I didn't. I mean, he gave her work with my name on it a D and my work with her name on it a B."

"So you fooled him."

"But he should have known that poem was mine."

"Then he gave you a B."

Maloney regretted letting the young man into Kilmartin's office now that it seemed clear he only wanted to know about some game he had been playing. He took the papers from Arne and put them back in the drawer.

"You'll get this back eventually."

But the blond giant seemed to have lost interest. He left, not closing the door, and after a moment, Maloney scrambled from behind the desk. He didn't want anyone looking in and seeing him there, as if he were trying to make contact with the dead.

He closed the office door and looked slowly around the all but empty room, trying to conjure the presence of Martin Kilmartin. He believed in life after death, didn't he? He had been raised to see his life as a prelude to eternity. That meant billions of souls were still in existence after their earthly trial and now Martin's was among them. He realized that he had never prayed for the repose of Martin's soul. Well, the wake and funeral were scheduled now and there would be many prayers offered for dear departed Martin Kilmartin.

9

FATHER CARMODY HAD A
'What did I tell you?' look when he came into
the viewing room at Paterson's where half a dozen sheepish mourners
clustered at a distance from the open coffin.

"What did I tell you?" Father Carmody said to Roger.

"Don't die in December."

The students were gone, many of the faculty were gone, the deceased himself was supposed to have been in Dublin when he was found dead in his Flanner office. Padraig Maloney, uncomfortable in a suit, had been cast more or less in the role of host of the affair.

"Are any family coming?" Roger asked him.

"They haven't answered the telegram."

"To whom was it sent?"

"He has a brother in Perth."

"Australia?"

"Is that where it is?"

Everything bore out Father Carmody's theory. The whole affair seemed ad hoc, unplanned, insufficient. Father Carmody volunteered to lead the rosary and took his place at the prie dieu before the coffin. The waxen visage of Martin Kilmartin was pointed toward the softly lit ceiling. There were floral arrangements, one of green carnations in the form of a shamrock, and what might have been an Easter candle burning at the head of the casket. Sauer slipped out before the prayers began and nearly bumped into a woman coming in. He actually cried out in surprise. It was Deirdre Lacey. Sauer changed his mind about leaving and followed her back in. From the prie dieu, Father Carmody began the rosary with the Apostle's Creed.

Throughout the rosary, a lengthy prayer, an Our Father followed by ten Hail Marys, repeated five times, the priest's authoritative voice contrasted with the reedy diffidence of the few mourners whose task it was to take up the second half of each of the prayers.

The human mind is naturally incapable of concentrating on one thing and distraction in prayer requires careful definition. The "booming, buzzing confusion" in our heads is at best brought under imperfect control by attempts to concentrate. So, in a species of distraction, Roger Knight thought during the recitation of the rosary, thoughts of the surprising presence of Deirdre Lacey competing with the insistent tone of Father Carmody's praying voice. When the prayer was nearing its close, someone took the chair beside Roger.

"I have to talk to you," Deirdre whispered. She looked at him with widened, frightened eyes.

"My brother will come pick us up."

She squeezed his hand and then left her hand on his. How chill and dry hers felt. Where had she spent the past five days? She tightened her grip on Roger's hand when she rose to go up to the casket. He accompanied her. Several times, she stopped but then she continued, collapsing onto the prie dieu when she got there. A great sob burst from her when she looked at Martin lying there all beautified in death, the man who had asked her to marry him, the man whom more than ever before she realized she truly loved. She wept there beside Martin's body for ten minutes. Father Carmody whispered in Roger's ear that his ride back to Holy Cross House had come.

"I'll see you tomorrow," he said in a stage whisper. He showed no curiosity in the weeping woman.

When Phil returned, Jimmie Stewart was in the van with him. The South Bend lieutenant did not react until Roger introduced him to Deirdre. Then he swung around in the passenger seat and stared at her.

"You're alive."

"Of course I'm alive."

But the tremor in her voice indicated that she did not find this as much a matter of course as her words suggested.

"Where to?" Phil asked.

"*Chez nous.*"

"Uh huh."

Deirdre said, "Definitely not *chez moi.*"

"I'll just go home, okay?"

"Good idea, Phil."

At the apartment, Roger made a huge batch of cocoa and bowls of popcorn, first having determined that Deirdre was not in need of a real meal.

"I have been living on junk food for days."

"Tell us about it."

Martin had made reservations for their flight to Dublin under the names of Jim and Norah Barnacle on Aer Lingus. The plan was to drive the car he had rented to O'Hare rather than leave her car in the long-term parking lot there for weeks. Deirdre was eager to get away from South Bend because Fritz was there, but she could not explain her anxiety to Martin.

"He was such a slowpoke!" But there was tenderness in the complaint. "He just would not get a move on. We were still at his place when the phone rang. While he answered it, I completed his packing. He came in to say we had to drop by his Flanner office."

"What for?"

"He said it had been Paddy Maloney who'd called to say that there was a gift for us on Martin's desk. I said we could pick it up when we came back, but he thought it might be something that wouldn't keep. I figured that even with this delay we would get to O'Hare in time to leave as originally planned."

When she finally got Martin out of his apartment and into the rented car, she drove to the campus. There was a fuss with the gate guard because the rented car did not have a university sticker, but he let them through and Deirdre pulled up behind Flanner. The doors of the building were locked because of the midsemester break and for a moment it seemed that Martin did not have the ID card that would get them in. But then he found it and soon they were rising through the silent floors to seven.

"I thought Professor Maloney would be there to meet us, since he had called, but the floor was deserted. There was nothing on Martin's desk. He found that funny but I was angry. If it hadn't been for that phone call we would have been on our way and out of this city." She did not have to say that what she meant was out of the reach of Fritz Davis. But thoughts of Fritz were very much with her.

Martin was looking through the drawers of his desk, saying they must have hidden it somewhere, when his telephone rang.

"It was so loud in the empty office on that empty floor that we both jumped. I stood frozen and then when he reached out for the phone I screamed at him to leave it alone and not answer it."

"Why not?"

"I had a premonition. And I was right. As soon as he began talking into the phone, his expression changed and he took several short breaths. And then he sneezed!"

The sneeze lifted him from his chair, his eyes met hers and then even as he stared at her the light seemed to go out inside him. He fell forward onto the desk.

"That's when I realized what I had been smelling since we got there. Pepper! And when I leaned over Martin to take his pulse I knew that the phone had been sprayed with pepper. There was no pulse. Suddenly I was terrified. I don't remember how long I stayed there, just turning from one wall to another, staring at Martin, knowing he was dead. And then I felt in danger myself."

She ran from the office, closing the door behind her and took the stairway to the ground floor.

"I almost continued to the basement, but then I heard voices down there and realized I was on the ground floor."

Before going out through the delivery entrance, she stood looking out the little window in the door to see if there were any signs of Fritz. Seeing none, she finally made a dash for the car.

"Where did you go?"

"To Niles. To a crummy little motel in Niles. Close enough to pick up South Bend stations and the *Tribune*."

Phil and Stewart had dozens of questions to ask her, and Deirdre answered as best she could, but Roger himself had to ask the only question that truly interested him.

"When Martin answered the phone, did he say anything?"

"He said hello."

"But was there any conversation?"

She thought about it. "He was listening as the sneeze came on."

"And someone was on the line?"

"Yes! I heard the phone hung up when I was feeling his pulse."

"Any idea who called?"

"I've been thinking about little else for days. We were only there because of Maloney's call."

Arrangements were made for Deirdre to spend the night in Melissa's apartment, which was close by.

"Your car was towed away by the police," Phil explained.

"Why?"

"The car of a missing person. We opened the trunk."

She turned to face Phil directly. "And it was empty?"

"Yes."

She turned away. "So he got it, after all."

"Fritz?"

She nodded.

10

PHIL SAT IN WHILE STEWART questioned Professor Padraig Maloney. It began as a summary of what had happened and what was known.

"You've got a visiting Irish poet, fragile as an egg, who announces his engagement to what, a graduate student?"

"Deirdre Lacey. A special student."

"Special."

"She is allowed to take courses but she isn't working for a degree."

"Is that rare?"

"Very rare."

"Who admitted her?"

"I did. As acting director of the program. With consultation, of course."

"When did she begin?"

"In August. The fall semester. She was a great admirer of Martin's from the beginning."

"Were you surprised at the engagement?"

"Surprised?"

"I gather Kilmartin was in very poor health."

"So he told us. But people like that often live forever."

Phil said, "Were you skeptical about his poor health?"

"How would I know? I took his word for it."

"Didn't his health come up when he was invited to come to Notre Dame?"

The professorial eyebrows lifted about the rims of his cloudy glasses. "Let's find out." He spun around in his chair and still seated walked his way to a file cabinet. He made a humming noise as he searched the drawer he opened. "Here it is!" He turned and walked his chair back to the desk. "Kilmartin's folder."

Stewart held out his hand. Maloney sat back, bringing his bearded chin to his chest. "Oh, this is confidential."

Stewart took a folded document from his pocket and handed it to Maloney. "I'll trade."

"What's this!"

"A search warrant. It covers the whole seventh floor."

"But you can't just come in here and, and . . ."

"We are investigating what may be a murder. I think that was your suggestion."

"I don't remember saying any such thing."

"Do you remember calling Kilmartin just before he was to leave for Ireland and telling him he must stop by his office to get a present from his colleagues?"

Silence fell over the room. Maloney looked from Stewart to Phil and back again. "You're accusing me?"

"I find that you and Kilmartin were rivals for the girl who ended up as his fiancée."

"I am not going to sit here and listen to this."

"Would you rather go downtown?"

"You'd arrest me?"

"I hope that wouldn't be necessary."

"I can't believe this."

"You can, of course, get a lawyer."

Maloney's injured incredulity only increased. Stewart laid out what had brought him to Maloney. The rivalry, knowledge of his fragile health, the call to Kilmartin, and the pepper spray on Kilmartin's phone.

"When the couple got to the office, they found no present awaiting them. The phone rang, Kilmartin answered. The pepper brought on the sneeze that took his life. Did you make that call?"

Maloney decided that he wanted a lawyer, after all. He put through a call to the main building and learned that the university counsel was in Florida. Like the rest of the campus, the main building was depopulated during the midsemester break.

"But I need a lawyer. The police are here demanding to look at confidential records."

A young lawyer named Laxalt was holding down the office during this fallow period. He responded with the zeal of the young, telling Maloney to say nothing until he got there. So for nearly fifteen minutes the three men sat in Maloney's office awaiting the arrival of Xavier Laxalt. Phil took his cue from Stewart, who sat in calm silence during this hiatus. Finally a youthful face looked in.

"Professor Maloney?"

"Are you Laxalt?"

"I am. And who do we have here?" he said to Stewart.

As a rough guess, Phil would have placed Laxalt in junior year of high school. He was short, blond, and had the look of a choirboy. Stewart told him the purpose of his visit.

"You're arresting Professor Maloney?"

"Well, the idea was to take him downtown for questioning."

"That would be the equivalent of arrest—from the point of view of perception."

"Now that you're here, why don't I just go on with my questions?"

First Laxalt took Maloney out of the room, where their exchange was audible but not intelligible. Phil took the opportunity to hand Stewart the note Roger had received. Roger had advised using it or not at Phil's discretion. Maloney's attitude made the decision easy. The note was unsigned, in capital letters and printed on a laser printer.

THERE IS A KEY TO KILMARTIN'S OFFICE IN MALONEY'S.

Stewart read it, looked at Phil, folded the paper and put it into his pocket. Maloney and Laxalt entered stage left.

"I reserve the right to stop these proceedings at any time," the lawyer said.

"So do I," Stewart replied. "All right, this is why we're here. Professor Maloney resented the popularity and fame of Martin Kilmartin. He had pursued Deirdre Lacey and lost her to Kilmartin. When Kilmartin and his fiancée were about to leave for their flight to Dublin, Maloney persuaded Kilmartin to come by his office here to pick up a going-away present. There was no going-away present in the office. While they were in the office the phone rang. Kilmartin answered it and the pepper with which the phone had been sprayed brought on the fatal sneeze."

Maloney laughed. "First, I did not call Kilmartin and ask him to come to his office."

"His fiancée says otherwise."

"She is wrong."

Jimmie Stewart got out the note Phil had given him and handed it to Maloney, but Laxalt intercepted it. He read it, then showed it to Maloney. Again Maloney laughed. "Of course there are keys to the offices here. But the dean has keys as well. So does campus security. I think the maintenance man of this building has keys—at least he can get into all the rooms. So can the cleaning ladies."

"Let me see your copy of Kilmartin's key."

Maloney looked at Laxalt, who gave his assent. From a drawer, Maloney got out a box of labeled keys. He went through them casually the first time, then he spilled the box onto his desk and examined them all again. He looked at Laxalt. "It isn't here."

"I wonder what happened to it," Stewart said in tones meant to infuriate.

"Oh come on," Laxalt objected. "Professor Maloney is as surprised as you are."

"But I am not surprised."

Stewart fished a plastic baggie from his jacket pocket and held it up. In it was a labeled key—721—the number of Kilmartin's office.

"Where did you get that?" Maloney demanded.

"From the glove compartment of your automobile." Stewart slid open the bag and held it toward Maloney and Laxalt. "Perhaps you can detect the smell of pepper?"

11 ⟶ MELISSA WAS AT FIRST SKEPTI-
cal and then annoyed when Arne told her what
he had done, e-mailing her poem under his name and vice versa, to
test Martin Kilmartin.

"What a sneaky thing to do."

"It proved a point."

"Which is?"

"For some reason he didn't like me, and I think we know what
the reason was."

"Oh, for heaven's sake." But the corners of her mouth dimpled in
the beginnings of a smile. A smile that could have been a prelude
to tears when she remembered that Martin Kilmartin was dead. Melissa could count the number of dead people she had seen—her
grandfather, a classmate in high school who had been killed in an
accident. But she had never known them in the way she had known
Martin Kilmartin. At the wake she had sat stunned, in the back, out
of sight of the Knight brothers. She had seen Deirdre come in before
anyone else noticed her and it was like seeing a ghost. She realized
that she had assumed that Deirdre too was dead.

"Melissa, he gave your poem a D because it had my name on it.
And mine got a B because he thought it was yours."

"What poem did you submit?"

"I only wrote one."

"Melissa?"

"I didn't call it that." He looked away. "I called it Love Poem."

"And it had that line?"

He turned back to her and nodded.

"You dope, do you think he forgot that line? After spending a whole class on it? Obviously your little joke didn't fool him a bit."

"Then why did he give yours a D?"

"That's probably what it deserves. Arne, neither one of us is likely to become a poet. Tell me, how did you find out about those marks?"

"I asked Professor Maloney to let me into Kilmartin's office."

"And he did?"

"I had to talk him into it."

Melissa was more shocked by this than she had been by Arne's silly little trick. Maloney had a key to Kilmartin's office and he had used it at least once since the murder, when the office was still technically sealed off as a crime scene.

Maloney was no comfort and Arne had become a stranger by what he had done. Brian had gone home to Midlothian and then joined his brother's family in Sarasota. Melissa had only Roger Knight to turn to, and she did not do so reluctantly. Suddenly he seemed just the one to talk to in her present confusion.

"Do you think someone caused Kilmartin's death?"

"Whoever sprayed pepper on his telephone and then called him up—assuming they are the same person."

"They would have to get into a locked office to do that."

"Locks have keys."

She wanted so much to tell him then what was weighing on her mind. But when she learned what Deirdre had said about Maloney's call to Martin just before they were to leave for Chicago all reluctance left her.

"He couldn't have lost his key and gotten into his office that day."

"No, he still had his key to 721." Roger had made popcorn when she arrived and poured her a root beer. Phil was listening to a game in the next room. Despite the fact that Phil was a private detective, and that Roger had helped him on his cases, there was a peacefulness in the apartment that made thoughts of one person plotting to take the life of another seem unreal.

"Having a key of one's own gives, I have learned, only an illusion of privacy, at least so far as institutions go. A professor is assigned an office and given keys and doubtless thinks that he alone has access to his lair. But think of it. Each morning he arrives to a clean and sparkling office. Someone has been in to make it that way, the cleaning ladies. The custodian of the building has a master key, something you learned when Kilmartin's body was discovered. What is that fellow's name?"

"Branigan. Yes, he has a master key. But a funny thing. The other day Mrs. Bumstead called on him to open her office and he came upstairs and found his master key was missing. Luckily, I came along and was able to let her in with my key."

"But normally he would have one. Campus security also has the right and ability to enter locked offices under certain circumstances. So there are many ways a private office is less than private. One thing we can rule out, however."

"What?"

"That someone could have a copy made. No key maker would copy a Notre Dame key. I speak of course of those in the vicinity."

"But it is physically possible. I mean, a key maker could make a copy if he wanted to."

Roger nodded. "So we cannot rule that out. The problem with the locked-door mystery is that there are too many keys to the lock."

In a way this made it easier for Melissa, but even so she chose to convey the fact to Roger by an anonymous note rather than just tell him. THERE IS A KEY TO MARTIN'S OFFICE IN MALONEY'S. It was only the day after he received the note that Roger mentioned it to her.

"A correct but potentially equivocal use of the apostrophe. The word 'office' is understood after 'Maloney's' of course but most people would have made that explicit."

"So it's saying that Maloney had a key to Martin's office."

"That is why he was arraigned today and is at large only because Xavier Laxalt arranged bail." Roger told her of the key to Kilmartin's office that had been found in Maloney's glove compartment.

"Do you think he did it?"

"Well, he could have. Lieutenant Stewart makes it sound plausible that a jealous Maloney exacted a cunning revenge. But I can understand why Laxalt dismisses the charge as unprovable. It isn't as if a can of pepper spray were found in his briefcase."

"Did they look?"

Roger was about to toss a handful of popcorn into his mouth but stopped. "Phil," he called. "Did they check out Maloney's personal effects?"

"No physical evidence was found. Apart from the key."

"Not even in his briefcase?"

"I don't remember Jimmie mentioning a briefcase. I'll ask him tomorrow."

"Tomorrow?"

"All right, all right. Wait till there's a time-out and I'll call him."

Ten minutes later, Phil came in to say that Jimmie had not looked through the professor's briefcase.

"Who's winning?" Melissa asked him.

"We will. We're behind, but we'll win."

12

ALL THE WHILE DEIRDRE LA-
cey was missing, Branigan kept thinking of that
bearded biker at Fiametti's across the state line. And then when he
heard that a former husband of Deirdre had appeared in South Bend,
frightening her, Branigan thought he knew what had happened. It
was knowledge he would give anything not to have. He sure as hell
wasn't going to that lieutenant, Stewart, and tell him what he knew.
All he had to do was imagine doing that and he could see how full
of holes his story would sound.

Because his whole story turned on Fritz slipping the master key
from his ring in that minute or so when the buxom Millie was at their
table, blocking his view of the bearded biker. They'd ask if he was
sure he'd had the master key on the ring at the time? Yes. He had
just been showing it—and showing off—to Fritz, telling him what a
big shot he was because he could open any lock in Flanner. And
when did he first notice it was missing? Telling about not having the
key when he was asked to let Mrs. Bumstead into the office of Celtic
Studies would make him look like a bumbling fool. The more he
thought of it, his story showed what a jackass he was a lot more than
it pointed the finger at Fritz as the one responsible for Kilmartin's
death and the disappearance of Deirdre. And then Deirdre reappeared, back for the funeral of Martin Kilmartin.

Branigan stood in the back of Sacred Heart while the melancholy
service was held. There were maybe a dozen people in the pews, so
it was easy to notice Deirdre Lacey. Afterward, the casket was put
into the mortician's vehicle and the mourners followed it on foot as
it drove slowly to Cedar Grove Cemetery, where the body would be

kept pending a decision on whether or not Kilmartin would be sent home to Ireland for burial. That done, there was a reception in the lobby of the McKenna Center, and Branigan helped himself to the food, more or less ignored until Stewart came over to him.

"What's this about losing your master key?"

"Who told you that?"

"It was mentioned when we were tracking down those who had access to his office."

"I lost it, yes."

"Was it the replacement key you got from campus security that you used to open Kilmartin's office when the body was found?"

He nodded. "I still haven't found my own key."

"I suppose it'll turn up."

"I hope so."

Branigan felt relief when Stewart left him.

Later that day Branigan confronted Deirdre Lacey in the lobby of Flanner. He had been on the lookout for her since returning from the post-funeral feed, but when she arrived it was with Roger Knight, sitting next to him in his golf cart. Branigan watched them as they sat for a minute in the parked vehicle. Then Deirdre patted the fat man's arm and leaned toward him as if to be kissed, but he just smiled and nodded and she got out of the cart. She came alone to the entrance of Flanner, head ducked down against the weather. Branigan jumped forward and opened the outside door for her and then followed her to the elevator, where he got in with her. This did not startle her, perhaps because she was shivering from the cold. She had a white woolen cap pulled over her head. Only when she unbuttoned the coat did her black dress indicate that she was in mourning.

"Seven, right?"

"Yes."

"As the custodian of the building I know names but not all the faces."

He turned so that the plastic ID on his shirt was visible.

"Branigan. Well, I knew your face but not your name. I'm Deirdre Lacey."

"Oh, I know you." Halfway up he said, "I met Fritz Davis at a bar in Michigan."

"That figures." No surprise, no hesitation. She shook her head, mildly amused, and that was all. Branigan had expected a lot more reaction than that.

"I heard you were scared of him."

"Did you?"

"The campus has been full of rumors these past days."

"It looks deserted to me."

There was that in her manner that suggested she was the lady and he the menial and this exchange with him represented some kind of noblesse oblige. Branigan, who had convinced himself that he was as smart as any of these professors and in selected areas knew a helluva lot more than any of them, was irked.

"I think your husband Fritz stole my master key. When we met, I told him about my job and showed him the key. The next time I had occasion to use it, it was gone."

"My husband Fritz," she repeated. "Is that one of the rumors going about the campus?"

The car stopped and the door slid open. The seventh floor. Branigan followed her out. She stopped and looked at him impatiently.

"I think he stole my master key." Didn't she get it?

"Have you told the police?"

"Do you think I should?"

She looked at him. "Well, you're telling me."

"Look, I wanted to warn you. If the guy frightens you and if he's got a key to all the doors in this building, well, I thought you might want to take it into account."

She melted and put a hand on his arm. "I'm sorry. Of course. And I'm grateful." She hesitated. "Look, wait while I check my office and I'll go down with you."

"I'll come with you."

She opened the door and flicked on the lights as she went in. The switch might have turned on her scream. She backpedaled into Branigan's arms and over her shoulder he saw the body sprawled across the floor. Branigan stepped around the young woman, who was babbling nonsensically, and looked down at the body. At first the beard made him think it was Fritz Davis, but when he eased the body over he saw it was Padraig Maloney. The cord of the telephone was still tight about his neck. But as the body of Deirdre went limp in his arms, Branigan heard a groan from Maloney.

13

"I WOULD HAVE COME DOWN for the funeral if only I had known in time, it's just an hour from Midlothian."

Donald Weber stood in Roger Knight's office, wringing his hands and emitting a kind of keening sound.

"I didn't realize you knew Martin Kilmartin that well."

"I didn't know him at all. That's just the point. It's a matter of institutional solidarity." Weber inhaled and then took the chair Roger had been urging him toward since his unexpected arrival. "The formality is all the more important when it is a question of someone like Kilmartin."

"I don't understand."

"Well," Weber said, and sighed. "How can I put it so you won't find it offensive yourself?"

There was, Weber opined, a Notre Dame of legend, of tradition, of fierce loyalty. "The Notre Dame of which Malachy O'Neill was the epitome. Jim Elliot understands that, give him credit. He knows that in order for Notre Dame to go on being Notre Dame it has to develop within its tradition. Now what in hell do people like Sauer and Becky What's-her-name have to do with that? They would be equally happy or unhappy at Meatball Tech, provided the salary was as astronomical as here."

What Weber meant was that there was excellence and then there was Notre Dame excellence. What he objected to was substituting generic excellence—conceding that was what the university was getting with these clowns, a questionable thesis Weber seemed ready to rebut—and an excellence peculiar to Notre Dame.

"And Martin Kilmartin?"

"Exactly! He could be the best poet Ireland ever produced and not be right for Notre Dame."

"Did you know Yeats visited Notre Dame twice?"

For a moment, Weber was angered by what he took to be an irrelevancy, but then he smiled and nodded vigorously. "Exactly! I see what you mean. Nowadays they would try to hire him."

"Wouldn't that have been a coup?"

"No! Look what's happened to football."

"Football?"

Weber was patting his chest in an exploratory way and now brought out a crushed package of cigarettes. "Can I smoke in here?"

"Go ahead."

"A smoke-free campus," Weber muttered as he bent over the match he'd lit. "I'll bet Father Sorin used snuff."

Smoke, inhaled deeply to sully his lungs, now poured from Weber's mouth in accompaniment to a sigh. "God, that tastes good." He examined his cigarette. "Unfiltered Camels. They're harder to get than cocaine."

"You were going to say something about football."

"Well, it's obvious, isn't it? When did the team begin to sink in the national standings? When we began to recruit the same kids every other place was after. Generic excellence. How did Notre Dame recruit when it was great? The Catholic high schools of Chicago, the parishes of Pennsylvania. There was a whole network of volunteer scouts who alerted the coaches to a hot prospect, a Notre Dame prospect."

"Well, you have a unified theory, certainly."

"It's a fact, not a theory, Roger. The theory has to do with why they act like this."

"Have you spoken of this with anyone here?"

"What's the use? Sauer thinks Malachy O'Neill is a joke. The institutional memory is disappearing. Look at you."

Roger laughed. "I try not to."

"I'm serious. You're good. I believe that. You wrote an interesting monograph or . . . you know the guy."

"Baron Corvo."

"Right. So what does that have to do with Notre Dame?"

"Malachy O'Neill was interested in Corvo, it turns out."

"Who says so?"

"He began an essay on Corvo's work." Roger laughed. "He called it 'Someone to Crow About.' "

"I don't get it."

"Corvo means crow."

"I never heard O'Neill mention such a person."

"You might find the newly discovered O'Neill papers interesting."

Weber narrowed his eyes. "Will they go into the center Elliot wants to fund?"

"Eventually, I'm sure they will."

"Have you accepted the offer?"

"To be director? No."

"Are you being coy or are you serious?"

"Obviously I couldn't be anything but serious about such an offer."

"But you won't accept it?"

"I haven't decided."

"Not deciding is a decision. You don't want it. You have an instinctive sense of how wrong it would be."

"I may not be the man for the job, that's true. But who is?"

"I am!"

Weber leapt to his feet as he said it. He repeated it. He leaned toward Roger as if willing him to agree. This, clearly, was the point of Weber's visit.

"Recommend me. Jim wouldn't think of me if someone doesn't suggest it to him. We're too close. We've known one another too long. He is, to be frank, a bit jealous of me."

"Ah."

"Because I was there in the class when Malachy O'Neill departed this earth. Jim thinks that makes me one-up on him. But think of the symbolism. I am there, a graduate student, when Malachy breathes his last."

Weber saw it as an analogy with the upper room where tongues of fire had settled over the Apostles, filling them with courage and zeal.

"It was a Pentecost," Weber said in hushed tones. "A confirmation."

A moment of silence during which Weber lit another unfiltered Camel.

"Will you tell Jim this is the thing to do?"

"I will talk to him," Roger said carefully.

The words catapulted Weber to his feet and he leaned over the desk. Without that impediment between them he might have tried to kiss Roger. As it was, he grabbed his hand and began to slobber over it.

"I'll never forget it. Who else is there? Kilmartin is dead."

It seemed unwise to point out to Weber that he had not promised to recommend him. Weber had heard what he longed to hear. Roger was now his advocate.

"He'll do anything you say. He admires you. Really admires you. That's why he made you the offer. His motives are right. All you have to do is direct them to another and more appropriate candidate."

Ten minutes later, Weber got up to go. He opened the door that led to the parking lot and stood looking out at the campus.

"God, I love this place. I'd kill to get back here."

14 MELISSA WAS GETTING OFF THE
elevator when the gurney bearing Padraig Ma-
loney was wheeled out of the west pod of the seventh floor of Flanner.

"What's happened!"

Deirdre was in the little band accompanying the medics who had
come for Maloney, but she turned and went back toward her office.
Branigan got into the elevator with the medics and Melissa squeezed
in next to him. Maloney was on his back and his beard had been
cropped to reveal his throat. He groaned. An eye opened and he saw
Melissa. His hand groped for hers.

"Tell me what happened."

"Leave him alone," a medic said. "He shouldn't talk. His throat's
a mess."

Another groan. Melissa took Maloney's hand in both of hers and
began to rub it, as if restoring the will to live. Maloney looked up at
her with infinitely sad eyes and tears began to well up in them. It
was all Melissa could do not to take him in her arms and comfort
him.

In the lobby of Flanner, Maloney was wheeled out the back way,
Branigan watched him safely aboard the 911 vehicle, then turned to
Melissa. "Someone tried to strangle him."

"Dear God."

"Either that or he tried to commit suicide."

It said something about recent events and her reaction to them
that Melissa found herself almost calmly weighing these alternatives.
In favor of the second was that Maloney was his own worst enemy.

"What hospital will they take him to?"

"St. Joe's."

In the manner of hospitals nowadays, what now called itself somewhat grandly the St. Joseph Medical Center had risen from the ashes of its previous selves so that only an archeologist could tell from its outside what was new and what was old. The receptionist in Emergency sat behind what looked like bulletproof glass and had to be addressed through a speaker. In a sitting room a dozen woebegone people who looked like Dante rejects stared despairingly at a television set where some mindless game was being played with shouts and screams and manic smiles. To the left of the reception desk, glass doors slid open for medical personnel then shut behind them, coming or going. Melissa sailed through after a pair of blue-clad nurses, her back tingling in expectation of being challenged. But no one said anything and she walked slowly down the corridor, looking into the examination cubicles where patients seemed to have been abandoned to their own devices. And then she saw what was left of Padraig's beard and pushed through the half-drawn curtain. His eyes opened, then closed in shame.

"Now tell me what happened," she said.

He groaned.

"Who did this to you?"

"Someone who wanted me dead."

The curtain was swept aside and a doctor and nurse entered. They ignored Melissa. The doctor stood next to Padraig, consulting a report the nurse had handed him. He lifted Padraig's chin and looked at his throat. Before he touched the raw red line he donned rubber gloves, then his unreal fingers palpated the throat.

"Can you talk?"

"More or less."

He listened to Padraig's chest, put a thermometer between his whiskered lips, looked at Melissa and said, "He'll be all right."

Melissa realized she was holding Padraig's hand. They assumed she was a relative, perhaps his wife.

His examination done, the doctor lifted his face to the ceiling, expelled air, and said, "Release him."

Padraig seemed about to protest the return of freedom but the doctor swept from the room while the nurse opened a locker in the corner revealing Padraig's clothes.

"Will you help him dress?" the nurse asked.

"Would you?"

Surprised and then annoyed the nurse said, "Why don't you wait outside?"

It was important not to get too close to the glass doors because they slid open automatically at anyone's approach. It was ten minutes before Padraig came slowly out of the cubicle, supported by the nurse. Miss Efficiency.

"You check out here."

She steered Padraig to a table where a very fat woman sat. "Medicare?"

"What?"

"Are you insured."

"I teach at Notre Dame."

"Do you have your Cigna card?"

He found it tucked away with a dozen cards in his wallet. The card activated the woman, who began plinking away at her computer keyboard, one eye on the insurance card. Forms were printed out, lines pointed to where Padraig must sign or initial. It was like renting a car. And then he was free to go.

"They brought me here in an ambulance."

"I have my car," Melissa said.

"Deirdre is back."

"Oh good."

He looked at her abjectly. "I thought she was dead too."

15

ROGER TOLD GREG WHELAN
about the surprising visit he'd had from Donald
Weber because he couldn't tell Phil without triggering a renewal of
his brother's campaign to make him accept the directorship of the
proposed Malachy O'Neill Center. On reflection, Roger had found
some justice in Weber's excluding him from the authentic Notre
Dame.

"He seems to think Malachy O'Neill was a paragon of every intellectual virtue. Of course, he hasn't seen the papers."

"Or the ballad."

"Ah, the ballad."

Martin Kilmartin had sinned on the side of kindness in likening
The Ballad of Pearl Harbor to Chesterton.

"Closer to Father O'Donnell?" Greg asked.

"Very much closer, if so good."

Charles O'Donnell, C.S.C., had been a dear man, a good priest,
an effective president of the university, and a poet. But what kind of
a poet? How many kinds of poet are there? Roger remembered Willa
Cather's essay on Sarah Orne Jewett, someone the novelist had known
and admired and whose writing she praised. But she did not over-
praise it. She had found a place for it in the commodious mansion
of literature, a modest place, but a secure foothold nonetheless. Could
something like that be said of Charles O'Donnell? There was a handful of poems that were genuine, good of their kind, indeed excellent
within their limitations. Had O'Donnell shown Yeats any of his poems
when he acted as the visiting Irishman's host? The diffident smile on
O'Donnell's face when he was photographed with the formally dressed

poet about to speak to the students of the university did not suggest that he imagined himself to be a peer of Yeats. Yet some few of his poems were as good as some of Yeats, though none approached the Irishman's greatest poems. Willa Cather had managed to praise her friend both honestly and sincerely. The same could be done with Father O'Donnell and Malachy O'Neill.

"Roger, when do you speak with James Elliot?"

"In a few days."

Greg said nothing, but the silence was a question.

"I don't know, Greg. I don't. But my inclination is to say no."

"It is a great opportunity. An unprecedented one."

Such ideas shimmer and glitter most as ideas, as possibilities, but what would such a center look like in reality? It might seem a monument to nostalgia and mediocrity. A director would have to defend the assumptions of founding a center in honor of Malachy O'Neill. Donald Weber could do that, Roger had no doubt. But then Donald Weber could adopt the opposite view just as easily, and doubtless would when he was disappointed in his ambition to be director. What Roger knew of James Elliot's view of his old classmate made it seem impossible that Weber should be rescued from the obscurity of Midlothian College and given the plum of the new center.

"Will you mention Weber?"

"I said I would tell Elliot of his visit."

Greg looked alarmed. "Is there any chance that Elliot would . . ."

"Oh, I don't think so. In fact, I am sure he would not."

"I would rather that there were no center at all."

David Simmons took Roger to lunch at a Chinese restaurant and came none too subtly around to the proposed center.

"You have to take it."

The necessity applied to Simmons and the Notre Dame Foundation: from their perspective such an offer must be accepted, it was too much money to refuse, and the prospect of putting up another building on the already crowded campus was irresistible to the administration.

"There are many who would want such a job."

"Weber's been to see you, hasn't he?"

"He dropped by, yes."

"He is lobbying for the position. The one person he can't ask is Jim Elliot. Roger, if you don't take the job, I am afraid Jim will back away. We let him define his offer in terms of you being director, whether or not that was wise, and he could walk away with no questions asked if you turn him down."

"Who has Weber been lobbying?"

"Me for one, as if I could swing it to him. And the provost. Well, an associate provost. Do you know Weber has a niece in the registrar's office?"

"I think I did know that."

"She goes around after him, urging that he shouldn't be hired."

"He has a lot to commend him."

"Not when he's the one stating it."

Phil and Jimmie Stewart were discussing the strange case of Padraig Maloney, who had been found in Dierdre's office with a telephone cord twisted around his neck.

"Have you ever wondered if it could have been self-inflicted?" Stewart said, speaking as he always did for the record.

"Are you serious?"

"The examination in Emergency was ambiguous in its result. That he was very nearly strangled seems true. The medical report alone wouldn't raise any questions. It's Maloney's explanation of what happened that raises questions."

Why was he in Deirdre's office?

"Let's ask him."

"I just wanted to be there. To feel her presence." There was defiance in his tone, although he looked sheepish when he said it. "I am a very sentimental man."

"You were attracted to her?"

Maloney rubbed his chin as if urging his whiskers to grow in more quickly. "Of course."

"And she was going to marry Kilmartin?"

"Yes."

"But he was dead. Now she was free."

"What a terrible thing to say. I thought she was dead too."

"So you went into her office to commune with her spirit."

"Mock me if you wish."

"How did you get in?"

"There are keys to all the offices in the director's desk."

"So you let yourself in?"

"I did."

"And were attacked."

"I must have left the door open."

"And you must have seen who did it."

"Hardly more than a glance before I blacked out."

"Someone came in, picked up the phone, wrapped the cord around your neck and began to choke you and you saw nothing."

"I hadn't turned on the light."

"But this was daytime."

"Winter daytime. A dull gloomy day. He had a beard."

"You remember that."

Maloney bristled. "That is enough. I will answer no more questions. You have no right or reason to quiz me like this."

"I don't know. It's against the law to commit suicide."

It was becoming the received view that Maloney had staged an attack on himself, causing himself some harm, no doubt of that, but with no intention of killing himself. He wanted to create the impression that he had been attacked. Melissa tried without much success to cast cold water on that.

"He knows the police don't believe him. Martin was dead, Deirdre was missing, who had more reason to resent their marriage? Of course you must suspect him. He half-suspected himself. But if he were a victim too, attention would be turned elsewhere. Is that the idea?"

"If that is the effect he wanted, he certainly failed."

"That's why I believe him. If he tried to fake something like that, he would bungle it. You should be looking for his assailant."

"He mentioned a bearded man."

"I know, I know. He spoke of a case in Cleveland, Dr. Shepherd, a bushy-haired stranger. Nobody believed him either."

Jimmie Stewart and Phil, in chorus, ticked off the reasons to suspect Maloney of killing Martin Kilmartin, starting with the staged attack on himself. Obviously Maloney thought himself to be a logical suspect.

"But it makes no sense," Roger said.

"Why not?"

"Because of Deirdre. If he thought she was dead, it would be like throwing himself on the funeral pyre. If he thought she was alive, then he has no motive. If he was acting, the only audience he would be playing to was Deirdre. And he thought she was dead."

16

BRANIGAN SPENT AN HOUR AT
Fiametti's after work, still thinking he might
run into the bearded biker again. Or at least see him. Sometimes he
wondered if the guy really existed. But then he spotted the skinny
girl with the hair hanging to her bottom and waited for Fritz to show.
Instead the girl left. There was the sound of a motorcycle kicking in
and then she sailed through the lot toward the highway. Branigan felt
more relief than disappointment.

Sitting in his basement lair in Flanner, flaked out in his easy chair,
ignoring the issue of *Sports Illustrated* in his lap, he resolved to tell
the police what he knew about Fritz Davis and how he had lost his
master key to the Flanner locks. He was as certain as anything that
Fritz had taken it from his ring when Millie blocked him from view,
but how could he prove it? Meanwhile, the police seemed to think
that Professor Maloney was behind the thing. Well at least they were
onto a bearded man, even if it wasn't Fritz Davis.

The following morning, he unlocked his basement door and turned
on the light and there was Fritz Davis, standing with booted legs
apart and his arms hanging at his side.

"How did you get in here?" His voice trilled like a frightened
woman's. Fritz held up a key.

"You're right. It works. I opened the outside door and then came
down here to wait for you."

"What do you want?"

"That's the question I ask you. Millie says you've been looking for
me."

Branigan wanted to get out of there, but his legs wouldn't work in reverse. He went to his desk as if routine could somehow neutralize the scare of having this guy in his office. "I'm not looking for you."

"I thought maybe you figured out how you lost this." He tossed the key and Branigan flubbed the catch. It jangled on the concrete floor. "I thought maybe you might point the finger at Fritz."

Branigan looked at the key on the floor. It looked like an orphan, all alone, off his ring. He stooped to pick it up and Fritz caught him in the behind with the side of his boot. The kick actually lifted Branigan off his feet and he sprawled across the floor. He felt a booted foot press down on the small of his back. That took his mind off the pain in his rear. His wrists were bound before he even thought of struggling. His ankles were bound next and then he was flipped onto his back. Fritz looked down on him with an evil smile.

"What's the number of Deirdre's room?"

"Look on the first floor."

A kick in the side. "She's not on the first floor."

"There's a list of occupants on the first floor! Alphabetical."

"She under Davis?"

"Lacey."

"Don't leave," Fritz said and went out the door.

Branigan waited a minute and then managed to sit up. His ankles were bound with telephone cord. The instrument had been tossed into a corner and the lengthy wire that enabled Branigan to use the phone either at his desk or carried to his easy chair had been jerked free.

He began to work his ankles and wrists, more in frustrated anger than hope, and his bonds seemed to loosen. Telephone cord wasn't meant for such a purpose. Within a minute, he had his ankles loose enough to ease one foot shoeless from the wire. He stood and then, eyes closed, in order to concentrate, worked on his wrists which were out of sight behind his back. Within minutes he was free. He took the cord and put it back into the phone and into the wall jack and heard a buzz. But when he stared at the instrument, he didn't know what number to call. What was Stewart's number? Campus security? Ha. And then he thought of Roger Knight and began flipping through the university directory. He punched in the numbers carefully, aware that his breath was coming in great heaving exhalations. His eyes went to his door.

He played out line as he went to the door, making sure it was shut tightly, locked. Fritz no longer had the key. Or did he? It was not on the floor. Of course he would need it to get into Deirdre's office.

"Hello?"

"Professor Knight?"

It was. In a burst of words he tried to tell Roger Knight of his predicament. He had been beaten and tied up. Fritz Davis had gone up to Deirdre's room.

"Fritz Davis?"

"He stole my master key. He had it all along. He has gone up to Deirdre's office."

"Stay there," Roger Knight said, and hung up.

There are minutes in a man's life that seem as long as hours, even years. Cowering in his basement office, knowing his door gave him no protection against Fritz Davis, Branigan yet remained where he was like a mesmerized chicken staring at a line. Could he trust Roger Knight to sound the alarm? He thought of the fat professor in his golf cart letting Deirdre off in front of the building on the day of the funeral. Hardly a model of strength and agility. The phone was in front of him, and the directory, he could call others. But his mind was now filled with the closet in the corner. It seemed an island of security compared to the vastness of his office. He crossed the room, let himself in and then closed the door on darkness.

He felt invisible there in the closet. Who would look for a grown man in a closet? He refused to admit thoughts of his wife and children, unable to bear the thought that they might witness his humiliation. He could have wept when he remembered being kicked and bound and left lying on his floor by a bearded maniac.

My God, he had gone upstairs to Deirdre's office. It hadn't occurred to him to call and alert her. But Davis might have been there already by the time Branigan got free. These thoughts added to his sense of total inadequacy. He was a prisoner in the building of which he was caretaker. He had been manhandled by a half-human biker who was now doing God-knows-what upstairs. He had to do something. He turned the knob of the door and pushed. Nothing. He wriggled it, twisted it, pushed, shook it. Nothing. My God, he was locked in the closet. He slumped to the floor and, in the dark, wept.

17   ROGER HAD ALERTED PHIL AND
Jimmie Stewart when he received the call from
Branigan and then got to his feet, put on his huge winter coat, and
pulled its hood over his head. Carefully he went outside and across
the icy walk to his golf cart. Soon he was crunching through the snow
on his way to Flanner. The sound of a siren growing ever louder
suggested that his call had had the desired effect. When he got to
Flanner, cutting through by the North Dining Hall and then taking
the diagonal walk to the front door, he could see several patrol cars
clustered in the lot to the west of the building.

"He isn't there," Phil said, emerging from the stairway door when
Roger entered.

"How about Deirdre?"

As if in answer, the elevator doors opened and two police officers
came out with a struggling bearded man in a leather jacket between
them. He glared at the Knight brothers and then was hustled off
toward the back exit.

"Book him," Jimmie called after them.

"What's the charge?"

"Breaking and entering." Jimmie held up a key. "The guy had a
master key to the building."

Roger persuaded the two of them to accompany him down to Branigan's quarters. They weren't inside the room for a minute before the
muffled sounds from the closet drew their attention. The door opened
easily from the outside and a bedraggled Branigan stumbled into the
light.

Jimmie had Branigan tell his story first right there where the events had happened. He disconnected the cords from his phone to show what Fritz Davis had tied him up with. Jimmie's brows lifted, doubtless when he thought of Maloney's story about being attacked and nearly choked to death with the cord from the phone.

"Why didn't you report the loss of that key?"

"I should have. I was going to. They knew about it at campus security." But the thought of deflecting blame did not hold him. "My God, I wish I had. Maybe none of this would have happened."

The problem with that, Roger reflected after he had driven his golf cart back to the apartment, is that there were too many keys around, as Jimmie Stewart had already observed. And one had been found in the glove compartment of Maloney's car. The least puzzling thing of all was how anyone had gained access to the offices in Flanner.

The case against Fritz Davis built slowly in the following days. He was linked to the Dixie Motel by a timorous Plaisance, he had left his mark all over Deirdre's apartment when he tore it up, apparently looking for the money. The money that Deirdre had put in her car trunk and from which it had been taken.

"That's not true," Deirdre said, when Phil and Jimmie were going over events with her at the Knights' apartment. She had moved in with Melissa again and was only doors away.

"Oh, I put the money in the trunk and of course it wasn't there when you looked. But I had taken it and, when Martin and I went to Flanner that day, that awful day, I brought the backpack along and put it in my office. I thought it would be as safe there as anywhere."

"Where did the money come from?"

This was a touchy point. "He must have stolen it."

"Had he stolen before, when you were with him?"

"Yes."

Under Jimmie's gentle urging she came up with a town in Wisconsin where Fritz had held up a convenience store.

"He nearly choked the clerk to death. I talked him into just tying him up and getting out of there."

Jimmie checked out the town and sure enough such a robbery had occurred there seven years before. This had the effect of making Deirdre an accessory to the crime, but Jimmie didn't press the point.

Roger said, "You're not suggesting that he stole three hundred thousand dollars from a convenience store?"

"There were others."

Once her tongue was loosened, Deirdre told it all. There had been a veritable crime wave through Wisconsin and southern Minnesota as Frtiz built up their nest egg. Deirdre seemed not to realize that she was incriminating herself as much as Fritz Davis.

"So the three hundred thousand was accumulated loot."

Deirdre nodded. "Twice stolen, since I took it from him."

"Why?"

"Spite. Anger at the way he treated me. Mad at myself for being so stupid. I never spent a dime of that money. But I could never think of a way to get rid of it that wouldn't cause more trouble." She paused and a pretty smile momentarily rode her lips. "Oh, I guess it was a bit of a nest egg too." The smile went. "I had been wondering how I could tell Martin about it."

"But you never did."

"Oh no! I could never think of a convincing enough lie."

The postponed question had finally to be put, a question to which Jimmie had already obtained the answer.

"The days after you fled Melissa's, you went to Niles and stayed in a motel there?"

"I wanted to be close enough to South Bend to be able to hear the local news. It was so frustrating that there was nothing about Martin's death, I mean the how and why of it."

"You stayed at the Bluebird?"

Deirdre did a slow double-take. "Did I tell you the name of the motel?"

"And Fritz Davis was also staying there."

There are silences and silences. From the kitchen where he had been following this exchange, Roger became aware of the beating of his own heart. How in the light of this could Deirdre retain her role as injured bride-to-be?

"He told you that, didn't he?"

"Is it true?"

"Yes." Her voice was calm. Roger slipped out of the kitchen into the living room, insofar as three hundred pounds of human flesh can be said to slip from one place to another. Deirdre seemed paler than when she had first arrived. She sat primly on the edge of her chair, hands in her lap, looking in turn at Jimmie and at Phil.

"Tell me about it."

"I knew he had brought about Martin's death."

"Did he admit it?"

"I didn't accuse him! My God, I was living in terror all those days. The past came back to me as if nothing had intervened. And of course there was Bobbie."

"Bobbie?"

"His girl. My replacement, I suppose you could say. Had I been like her? That was the question that ate away at my insides. I imagine this vacant-eyed girl, looking dumbly at the television screen, reading magazines from the supermarket checkout counter, jumping when Fritz told her to jump. I tried to imagine Martin Kilmartin finding such a creature attractive and I could not. I began to think that God had spared him, taking him when he did."

"Did he carry you off to Niles?"

"Oh no, no. He followed me there, as I learned. After I had checked in, he and Bobbie came to the door of my unit, and before I could do anything about it, they had forced their way in and set up camp."

"What was the point?"

"The money. He wanted his money back."

"And you gave it to him?"

"I did."

"We can't seem to find it. Of course, he denies that there was any stolen money he knew about."

"Of course."

"Any idea what he might have done with it?"

"Have you found Bobbie?"

"Describe her for me, will you?"

"When you find her, you might ask her if they're married."

18 MELISSA HAD AGREED TO LET
Deirdre have the extra bedroom in the apart-
ment she shared with two other graduate students—each unit had
four bedrooms—in part because there seemed no way to refuse the
request when Philip Knight had made it. It was like doing a favor
for Roger. Deirdre she could tolerate at best. She had shared the
general female disbelief when Martin Kilmartin was drawn to her.
That this master of lyric excellence should find Deirdre attractive
went beyond the usual mystery of male/female attractions. Both a
literal and a metaphorical ocean separated the two, or so it seemed
to Melissa and Mrs. Bumstead when they discussed the matter.

"You know who is just as nuts about her," Prudence said, hunching
a shoulder at the door of the director's office behind which Padraig
Maloney ate his heart out for the attentions of Deirdre.

"Men. They are a mystery."

"There's not much mystery here," Prudence said, and narrowed
her eyes significantly.

"Oh, no, I don't think so."

At least she hadn't thought so until Prudence Bumstead suggested
it, but afterwards she found it consoling to believe that Deirdre's
appeal was to the libido, to the animal in men, and that, when sated,
would lead to her dismissal. Except that there was no diminution of
Martin Kilmartin's interest in the special student. Doubtless he had
never met anyone quite like her. Neither had Melissa.

"What did you do after getting your B.A.?" Melissa had asked.

"Came to South Bend."

"You mean you just got your degree?"

"I was a late student."

"What did you do before you went back to school, work?"

"A little. We traveled."

That's all. "We traveled." It suggested affluence, the leisurely circumnavigation of the globe to ward off boredom. Melissa didn't believe a word of it.

"Bunk," Prudence said, when Melissa relayed the information. "She's a honky-tonker."

"A what?"

"Eric? My son." This was the nineteen-year-old spook with green and yellow hair of whom nonetheless Prudence was proud. "He sees her in those places across the state line."

"You're kidding."

"It sounded far-fetched to me too. But I had him come in and take a good look and he said, yeah, that's her."

"Do you think she takes Martin to such places?"

The "places" in question were haunts of what snobs on the faculty would call the underclass, the misfits and losers of the world who gathered in the semi-lit places and drank and fought and raised hell.

"Not unless he rides a motorcycle."

"A motorcyle?"

"Eric called it a bike, but he didn't mean a bicycle."

"She goes there often?"

"I didn't say that. It isn't as if Eric hangs around such places."

Amazing. So amazing she talked about it only with Prudence Bumstead, retaining the fiction that Eric was an Eagle Scout who happened to peek into a den of iniquity and spot Deirdre and then withdrew immediately to report to his mother.

That had been just before Martin Kilmartin announced to the surprised celebrants at the faculty party that he intended to marry Deirdre. Melissa had learned not to knock Deirdre to Arne any more than she would have to the smitten Padraig Maloney.

So, when Philip Knight asked her if she could put Deirdre up in her apartment after what had happened to Martin, Melissa had said, sure, of course. And it had been no trouble. Deirdre almost immediately went off to bed, wanting the solace of sleep, and the next morning Deirdre was gone. But now she had returned and again Melissa was asked to give her refuge.

"Until my roommates get back anyway."

This time Deirdre was more company. She had been hiding in a motel in Niles during these past days.

"But I had to come back for Martin's funeral."

"Of course."

"It's so difficult to believe that any of this has happened."

Deirdre was Cinderella, returned to her humdrum world after a glimpse of a wholly different life. One thing they agreed on, whoever had attacked Branigan had earlier attacked Padraig Maloney.

"His mistake was being in my office," Deirdre said.

"What was Branigan's mistake?"

"Just knowing me is dangerous with Fritz on the rampage."

Not all that reassuring at the time, but then Fritz was arrested in Flanner and taken off to jail.

"Now it's safe to go home," Deirdre said.

19

THE FIRST CLASS OF THE second semester met on Tuesday in the third week of January. Those who had spent the holidays elsewhere returned to a campus where much had happened and stay-at-homes like Melissa and Padraig Maloney were kept busy recounting the events that had taken place between semesters on the all-but-deserted campus. Now that Fritz Davis had been arrested and brought before a judge for a preliminary hearing and a trial date set, the local paper and the campus *Observer* were able to employ their customary omniscience in discussing what had happened.

"The victim was on the faculty?" asked the cultural editor of Padraig Maloney.

"A visiting professor. From Ireland. A poet, a famous poet."

"Could you spell the name again?"

Maloney did so with little confidence that the reporter would get it right. She was a spare young student whose head kept tipping to the left as she wrote and whose expression, when she looked at him, was skeptical. Or it might have been her contact lenses.

"What was the cause of death?"

"Pepper."

The skeptical look grew puzzled.

"A sneeze."

"Come on."

Padraig elaborated but he had lost credibility. When the story appeared the emphasis was on the condescending appraisal of Kilmartin's verse by Professor Geoffrey Sauer. "A lovely singer of limited range."

With the basketball season heating up, Phil was relieved to have fulfilled his professional obligations. He had been hired by Deirdre to locate her husband and now Fritz was safely under lock and key.

"And is he her husband?"

"He never was. The licence of the man who presided at their wedding had expired. He had been replaced as Justice of the Peace but continued to perform weddings for some months. It was quite a scandal."

"I should think so."

"Has the money been found?"

A thirty-second time-out enabled Phil to answer. "Roger, just between you and me and the fencepost, I doubt there was any money."

"You doubt your client's word."

"Oh, I think there was a backpack and there may have been some money in it. But a biker going around with three hundred thousand dollars?" Phil shook his head and returned to the game.

Roger did the Sunday *Times* crossword according to private rules of his own, moving diagonally over the puzzle from the lower-left corner to the upper right, usually able to follow a jagged avenue as he went. Once he had confined himself to the Down clues, not taking any help from the Across, but that challenge had paled. The truth was that the Friday or Saturday daily puzzles, while smaller, were a greater challenge than the larger Sunday puzzle. And *The Observer* ran the daily puzzles. Alas, there was no Saturday edition, necessitating the purchase of the complete paper for the one thing worthwhile in it.

Distracted, he chewed on his ballpoint pen, and considered the consequences of doubting Deirdre's word. Suspicion had fallen on Padraig Maloney because Deirdre had said he called Kilmartin when they were about to leave for O'Hare and Dublin and persuaded them to detour by Flanner to pick up a going-away present in Martin's office. When they arrived, there was no present, but then the phone rang and Martin, by answering the phone, had brought on his death because the receiver had been sprayed with pepper. He had ridden the resultant sneeze into paradise. And who had made the call? Who but Padraig? Or so Deirdre had suggested. So much depended on her veracity. But if Deirdre was not to be believed, perhaps none of that had happened. During halftime, Roger pointed this out to Phil, with remarkable results.

"My first instinct was not to take the case, Roger. And I wouldn't have, if she hadn't had Notre Dame connections . . ."

"Of course, she may be telling the truth on all counts."

"The money too?"

"Who knows?"

Phil thought he knew. The following day he met with Jimmie Stewart, who was disinclined to complicate a case the prosecutor thought would be a walk in the park. They were prosecuting Fritz for assault and battery, unlawful entry. A possible charge of kidnaping was in the background, based on the forceful detaining of Deirdre in the Niles motel.

"And Kilmartin?"

Jimmie made a face. "I know, I know. But Jacuzzi the prosecutor says he couldn't make it stick."

"He'll be out in a couple of years."

"As far as Kocinski is concerned, my one remaining duty is to testify at the trial." Stewart's eyes closed as if to shut out the thought of his chief.

But Phil was not to be easily dissuaded from pursuing the thoughts engendered by Roger's remark about Deirdre's veracity.

"Jimmie, on her own account, she deserted her husband, or at least a man she thought she had married, taking with her the money they had stolen over a number of months. She wants us to believe that."

"You want her prosecuted for those robberies in Wisconsin and Minnesota?"

"I think she might have used Fritz one last time. Imagine if the two of them colluded to get rid of Kilmartin."

"Give me a break!" Jimmie cried, throwing up his hands. They were having a beer in a bar across from the courthouse that called itself a pub and where Guinness was on tap, flown in weekly from that little bit of heaven that fell from out the sky one day and nestled in the ocean in a spot so far away. Jimmie sought solace in the creamy foam of his glass.

But Phil stubbornly laid out the scenario that suggested itself. Fritz tracks Deirdre to South Bend, intent on recovering the money she stole from him. The sight of her softens his anger and she sweet-talks him into going off together. But first there is the impediment of Martin Kilmartin. Fritz is persuaded to spray the phone.

"I told you what Jacuzzi said about the pepper spray." Jimmie waved for another round. "But the biggest flaw is that they have no motive for killing the poet. If they want to run off together all they have to do is do it."

Phil was taken aback, and regretted not having run through the theory with Roger. Later, he told his brother about the collapse of his theory.

"But, Phil, they did have a motive."

David Simmons who had access to such confidential information and passed it on as confidential told Roger that Martin Kilmartin had made Deirdre the beneficiary of his university perks—an insurance policy, an admittedly still minuscule retirement policy and, besides, a bonus coverage from the Credit Union from which Kilmartin had borrowed money to buy his car.

"How much in all?"

"Several hundred thousand dollars. Where are you going?"

"To call Jimmie."

20

WHEN DAVID SIMMONS TOLD Roger of the arrangements Martin Kilmartin had made to leave money to Deirdre, this was only a bump in a conversation that drove toward the fund-raiser's point in coming to Roger's office.

"You said you would decide after the second semester began."

"Not a very precise deadline." Roger smiled, but Simmons was too tense for jollity.

"Have you made up your mind?"

"There is one more conversation I wish to have before I do."

"With James Elliot?"

"Good heavens no. I speak with him once a day. He is more importuning than you."

"Father Carmody?"

Obviously Simmons was seeking a clue as to who else might be pressured on behalf of Roger's acceptance of the directorship of the Malachy O'Neill Center of Catholic Literature.

"Father Carmody is my confessor, so of course we talk."

"Your confessor?" That cut off a possible avenue. Father Carmody would not violate the seal of the confessional even for the benefit of Notre Dame.

"Greg Whelan is all for your taking the position, you know."

"Have you talked with him?"

"It's a shame that so brilliant a fellow has such a terrible impediment."

Greg had told Roger that he had encouraged his own stammer

when Simmons, seeking ways of persuading Roger to take the appointment, called on him in the archives.

"If I can be of any help?" Simmons said now, fishing, fishing, but Roger gave him no clue as to the person he must yet talk to.

That afternoon he pushed away from the desk as it came on three o'clock, bringing the chair to a halt when he had a good view of the parking lot from his window. Below was his golf cart, beyond under snow-laden trees the grotto, and then the lake where ducks were busy keeping some open water against the gathering ice. The scene conduced to contemplation and for a time Roger forgot his expected visitor and what that visit might reveal.

The building in which his office was, once Brownson Hall, once the convent of the nuns who had baked and cooked and laundered for the nascent community of Notre Dame, had been used for a variety of purposes over the years. It had housed the Freshman Year of Studies when that brainchild of Emil Hoffman was an innovation and then had become Earth Sciences, the name it still kept for many though it no longer named anything under its roof. The building came stepwise down from the level of the church and main building to the level where Roger's office with classrooms above it was flush with the ground. As old a building as there was on campus, save for Old College overlooking the lake, it gave a sense of continuity with Father Sorin and the other pioneers who had brought this institution from improbable hope to achieved reality. A road from the grotto led toward the community cemetery where those heroes lay. The nuns were buried across the road at St. Mary's. Roger remembered his recent trip up that road in his golf cart with Greg Whelan beside him when they had visited the grave of the poet president of Notre Dame, Father O'Donnell. All but forgotten, like the person in his poem "For One Departed."

There is no memory of you
In rooms that were your own,

I labor to construct anew
The combination known
So well—to see you in that door,
Crossing familiarly this floor.

There was no one living now to conjure the memory of Charles O'Donnell, C.S.C., and yet he and all the others were present in spirit on this campus, all those giants of the past whom only some remembered now. It was one of the great attractions of James Elliot that he retained so sincere and fervent a memory of Malachy O'Neill.

In the parking lot a vehicle came creeping along looking for a spot and then swung into a vacancy. In a moment the door opened and Donald Weber stepped onto the snowy parking lot. He looked toward Roger's window but would not be able to see that his arrival had been observed. With a sigh, Roger pushed himself back to his desk.

There was the sound of stomping, Weber ridding his shoes of snow, and then the creaking of the ancient wooden floor as he came down the hallway. He stopped outside Roger's door. Half a minute went by before there was the knock.

"Come in, come in," Roger boomed heartily, and Donald Weber entered, still redolent of the bracing outdoors. His expression was one he might have fixed on his face in the hallway before knocking on the door. How to describe it. Obsequious, Uriah Heepish, mendicant.

"Good afternoon, Roger."

Meanwhile Weber unzipped his lined coat. Roger told him to hang it on a hook beside the door.

"Oh, I'll keep it on until I warm up." But beads of sweat stood on Weber's forehead. He sat and pressed back against the chair.

"You said you had made a decision. About the Malachy O'Neill Center."

"I have. You will be the first one I inform of that decision."

"Really?" Weber sat forward, beginning to smile.

"I have decided to decline the offer."

"You have!" Weber fought his smile into submission and adopted what must have been meant to be a look of incredulity, even indignation. "Are you sure you want to do that?"

"I mean that I will decline, but my intention is firm. It is of course a great honor, far greater than I deserve and certainly more than I could accept. You helped me see that."

"I did?"

"The last time you were here. I mean, in this office."

"What did I say?"

Roger reminded him, in some detail and more or less verbatim. Weber had pointed out the unfittingness of additions to the faculty like Geoffrey Sauer and Martin Kilmartin. "And of course myself."

"I meant no disrespect."

"I believe that."

Roger fell silent and Weber waited, his upper body beginning to move like a metronome, as if to urge Roger to continue. Finally he asked if Roger remembered something else he had said on that occasion.

"I asked you to recommend me for the center. Now, if you are certain you yourself cannot accept it . . ."

"I have spoken with James Elliot."

"And what was his reaction?"

"He agreed with me entirely."

Weber fairly beamed and Roger chided himself for being so cruel.

"We were of one mind that you would never do as director."

"But, you don't want it . . ."

"And you want it too much. You want many things too much. And you have done things for which it is unlikely you will ever be adequately punished."

"What the hell are you talking about?"

"Causing the death of Martin Kilmartin."

Weber sat back. "That is totally and completely absurd." But he seemed to be waiting.

"I wonder if I wasn't in a way your accomplice. Would you have known how fragile his hold on life was if I hadn't told you? I think

204

you knew from the beginning that I would not accept the offer of the center. And you expressed my reasons rather eloquently. My mistake lay in telling you what a fine director Martin Kilmartin would make."

"The man knew nothing of Notre Dame and cared less."

"He did not have your exaggerated devotion, no. But he judges truly. And he judges the same no matter who is his audience."

"I want that job!"

Roger shook his head.

"You don't understand what it is to love this place."

"I have begun to think that I understand that far better than you do."

"Did you call me all the way down here to tell me this garbage?"

Weber rose slowly to his feet and seemed to grow as he stood there, breathing through his nose, staring down at Roger with hatred.

"You fat sonofabitch. You dog in the manger. You . . ."

He had put his hands on the edge of the desk and now began to push, propelling desk and Roger with growing momentum toward the bookcase. The back of Roger's chair slammed into the bookcase and above him there was the rumble of an avalanche beginning. Weber clambered over the desktop, trying to get hold of Roger's throat. Just in time the door burst open and Phil and Jimmie Stewart rushed in.

EPILOGUE

MONTHS LATER, THE SNOW had gone at last, winter was past and the voices of ducks were heard on the campus. Canada geese stopped traffic as they crossed the lake road, and mallards led their little ones to water, feathery promises of renewal and continuation. Roger Knight and Melissa sat on a bench, looking out over the lake.

"He got off easy."

"Donald Weber?"

"No. Fritz Davis. Five years maximum."

"It would have been difficult to make the charge of kidnaping stick."

In the absence of Deirdre. She had disappeared, embarrassed no doubt by her inheritance from Martin Kilmartin now that her renewed association with Fritz Davis was known. He had followed her to the motel in Niles and held her prisoner, but Fritz, by his own account, which few were willing to credit, said he would have been happy just to reclaim the money Deirdre had stolen from him and bike on down the highway.

"Twice-stolen money," Phil said.

"Like refried beans," said Jimmie Stewart.

It was Jimmie's belief that Deirdre had taken the backpack full of ill-gotten gains with her to Ireland.

"Paddy Maloney is flying to Dublin during the midsemester break," Melissa said to Roger.

"Hope springs eternal."

"He'd better be careful," Melissa said. "His retirement is a good deal more sizable than poor Martin Kilmartin's."

"You've looked into it?"

"Oh, stop it." She leaned briefly against his arm. "I'm through with older men."

"Or vice versa."

She punched his arm. "Do you think Deirdre had arranged for Fritz to kill her intended husband?"

"How would she do that?"

"Take Martin to the office before they were supposed to go to O'Hare and fly to Dublin."

"You have been misled by believing Deirdre's earlier story."

"Shouldn't I?"

"No."

A moment of nobility had illumined Deirdre's soul. When Fritz located her, she had saved herself from his brutality by turning over the backpack filled with money. He was astounded that she had spent none of it. Unwisely, thinking he was now content with Bobbie, she confided in him the arrangements Martin had made for her. She took on the allure of an heiress and appealed to his greed. Deirdre fled both him and Martin.

"Martin!"

"Given the murkiness of her own status—she did not know she and Fritz had never really been married—and having come to admire if not love Kilmartin, she realized she could not be a wife to him. So she decided to part with both Fritz's money as well as the legacy that would be hers from Martin."

"But she got that."

"To her surprise. She thought it was contingent on their having married."

"Then what did happen to Martin Kilmartin?"

"Deirdre was not at her apartment when he came for her and, unable to locate her, he went to Flanner, hoping to find her hiding in her office, a too-timid bride. Fritz sought her in the same place when he realized she had run off again."

Melissa turned toward him on the bench. "Are you saying that Fritz then sprayed the phone with pepper and . . ."

"No, he didn't do that."

"Who did?"

"Donald Weber.

Weber had changed from raging bully to craven coward when Phil and Jimmie Stewart burst into Roger's office in the nick of time. Prompted by Roger, Weber blubbered his confession. He had removed Kilmartin as an obstacle to his ambition to be director of the Malachy O'Neill Center. He had sprayed the phone with pepper, having learned of the poet's fragility.

"And then telephoned him?"

"No. He had no idea Kilmartin was in his office. He did not know that Kilmartin planned to leave the country. If Martin had not come looking for Deirdre, if they had gone off to Dublin, the spray would have lost its effectiveness."

"So who made the call?"

Roger smiled sadly. "You are still in the grips of Deirdre's original story. There was no call. Kilmartin just picked up the pepper-sprayed phone to make a call. A fatal decision."

"If Weber confessed, why hasn't he been arrested?"

"The prosecutor does not think he could get a conviction. No doubt he is right. A jury would find the elements of the puzzle too hard to piece together."

"A perfect crime?"

"An unpunished one, perhaps. At least judicially."

Weber had resigned his post at Midlothian College. Roger had received the news from Brian Elliot. Roger no longer heard from the boy's father. James Elliot had decided he had been generous enough already to his alma mater. David Simmons found this temporarily devastating, but soon other affluent targets beckoned and he went on with his mendicant task. Doubtless James Elliot had derived some consolation from reading Malachy O'Neill's estimate of Weber's work, sent to him anonymously by Greg Whelan.

"You must come for supper." Roger said when they rose from the lakeside bench.

"Not tonight," Melissa said. "I have a date."

"Aha."

"Arne Jensen."

"A younger man?"

"Let's just say not an older man."

The following week a waif named Bobbie was arrested while driving a motorcycle Fritz had reported stolen. In the saddle bags was found the now thrice-stolen money Bobbie had ridden off with. Her fate was unsettled. It seemed that she was only sixteen years old.

Spring came as it annually does, birds sang and the sweet smell of early flowers filled the air. As Roger directed his golf cart up the road from the grotto, squirrels scampered about and overhead the branches of the great trees that formed a tunnel over the road rustled confidentially. At the community cemetery Roger got out of his cart and moved slowly among the graves until he found that of Charles O'Donnell. There was no admonition to the horseman that he pass by, as there was on the grave of William Butler Yeats in far-off Ireland. There wasn't much traffic of any kind under the rustling trees where row after row of simple crosses marched away from the grave of Edward Sorin toward a future none of those who lay here would ever see but which would not have been possible without them. Roger prayed for them all and hoped that they in turn would remember the overweight Huneker Professor of Catholic Studies. He said as well a prayer for Martin Kilmartin, fragile poet, and for the repose of the soul he had sneezed away one winter day.